Earl in the
Yellow Shirt

Earl in the Yellow Shirt

A NOVEL

Janice Daugharty

HarperCollins*Publishers*

HarperCollins books may be purchased for educational, business, or sales promotional use. For information please write: Special Markets Department, HarperCollins Publishers, Inc., 10 East 53rd Street, New York, NY 10022.

FIRST EDITION

Designed by Ruth Lee

ISBN 0-06-018750-6

97 98 99 00 01 ❖/RRD 10 9 8 7 6 5 4 3 2 1

*In memory of my brother Elmo Staten,
whose artistic attempts continue to be
tried by my character Alamand*

Dedication to
LARRY ASHMEAD

Imagine that you wake early, go to your computer, work a couple of hours in sunlight streaming through silent windows. Imagine that your editor calls around nine and says he will buy your latest novel: "*Earl* is a step above anything you've written." That bright voice softened by morning.

Ten years of wrenching stories from the gut that nobody wanted, ten years in search of an editor (any editor would do!) and now Larry Ashmead. None love Larry so much as this grateful writer, who can write now without anguishing over what will happen to her next book.

PART ONE

PART ONE

Loujean

_ _ _ _ _ _ _ _ _ _ I hear Earl and my three brothers dragging their feet up the boardwalk off Troublesome Creek. You can tell the old man hears them too, the way he cocks his bony head and eyes the door, priming up to say to them what he's been saying to me all morning: Me and your mommer's done with one another, y'all do what you want to about hit. "Hit" meaning "it," and "it" meaning put Mama away decent or any way we can.

Buck sidles in first, shrunk-faced and scrunched against the cold, and Earl and Pee Wee and Alamand shove in behind him. Alamand has to pick up on the door to ram it shut against the wind. He don't get it closed good before a transfer truck revs up at the crossing and roars down the creek dip, grinding gears. The wind and racket scours the room of festering steam and clock ticks, but I can still smell the baby like a new puppy.

Mama didn't make it.

I know the boys have been to the funeral home in Jasper, Florida, since Earl's got on his light yellow shirt with his brown hair water-slicked. They make a place on the couch and perch like birds on a light line. The red rose curtain behind is pinned together with a clothespin and puffs at their backs. (That window's *been* busted out from where Buck drove the old man's head through it.)

"Well, Old Man," says Buck, sucking on a cigarette and squinching his hazel eyes. "Looks like they ain't no making the undertaker bury Mama less'un we can come up with a couple hundred." Smoke snorts from his long, crooked nose.

"Me and your mommer's done with one another," says the old man, "y'all do what you want to about hit." He rares back and jerks his sucked-hide face to the wall. One giant hairy ear stays tuned in, like he don't want to miss the solution even if it ain't his problem.

Pee Wee, my middle brother, hoves up and rakes his fingers through his shingled brown hair. "Hell, looks like a man in his line of work wouldn't lord it over poor people cause they ain't struck it rich yet!"

Then Buck starts. "We ain't got no choice but to go to Buster and see if the county won't . . ."

"I hain't listening to no sech!" The old man rocks to his feet, bellering and stomping on a weak floor joist. Every dish in the piesafe sets in dinging.

Mama's last baby don't make a peep. I can feel it warm up next to my leg on the bed. I can't hear it breathing. The covers don't move. I lay my hand on its back and feel its heart like a bitty chick's blood pulse. They're really getting into it now, Buck and the old man, over where they gone get the money from. The old man's going on about how none of his'n ain't never been put away by the county since Buster took it over, and how he ain't fixing to start looking to the county now. Buck's riled good—he's the oldest, going on twenty-eight, and like Mama always said, a worrywart.

Pee Wee is walking the floor, cussing. His keen face is kerosene yeller. Smells like he's done made a stop by The Line on his way back from the undertaker's where Mama's laying a corpse. He don't generally get into none of their scraps if he ain't drinking. Bout as big around as my leg from doing without so he can get the most out of his likker.

Alamand, setting on the couch next to Earl, goes to wringing his hands and chewing on his top lip. He's a mite on the chunky side with a white dish face and dark hair that curls up where his cap goes. Takes everything to heart, the sweetest one of the bunch. Was born with a double veil, according to Mama, is how come he can draw. I can tell he's itching to get on over to Aunt Becky's old house, where he can set and draw by hisself. Bad about stealing my pencils. He's the least one, or was until night before last. Fourteen years old, two years behind me in school when he goes.

"Looks like old Loujean there's just setting taking it easy," Earl says. His milky blue eyes snag mine. Up to now, he's been tapping his boots on the floor with his elbows ditched on his knees.

"Earl," I say, "chunk a piece of wood on the fire, will you?" I fix my skirt so my legs don't show. He twists around with one knee on the couch and parts the curtain to where it fans over the back. Out of respect for me, he raises the window where he could of reached right through the head-size hole in the glass.

I wish I could go out. I wish I could leave this baby where she lays and go outside. I gaze through the gapped curtain at the shed sweetgums on Troublesome Creek, where the wind sings lonesome in the tents of tangled vines. White as bleached lace on the tin sky.

Earl grabs a stick of firewood off the scaffold and lets the window down and fixes the curtain back, just so. Then, trying to look real handy, he struts over to the stove and flips open the door latch with the toe of his right boot. Smoke boils out and eats up my eyes.

The firelight on his pale square face makes him look scalded, his milky eyes bright. He rubs his hands together over the pot of steaming lima beans and grins at me. The fire cracks and pops and the stovepipe roars, turning red as my face.

"Prechate it," I say. Feels like me and Earl's the onliest ones in the room, but that good feeling ain't enough to keep my mind off of my troubles. I won't make it to school today—it's Friday anyhow—pro'bly not never no more. But that's all right.

Earl backs to the stove, bowing his stocky chest, and rocks with his hands latched behind. I can smell his britches scorching. When it looks like he can't stand the heat no more, he taps back over to the couch and plops, eyeballing me around Pee Wee and Buck walking the floor and fussing with the old man. Old Man ain't moved, but he's study quarreling. Where he's bald on top, a sprig of gray-glazed hair sticks up like a scared man's in the funny papers.

"Buster and that bunch over yonder at the courthouse hain't never took no interest in me and mine," he says.

"If you'd had ery lick of sense," pipes up Buck, "you'd a done like Buster told you when Aunt Becky died, stead of puffing up and taking it on yourself to put her away fancy." Buck's preaching to the old man now, gulping between words like a Hardshell Baptist, with his hip cocked. "Now we left owing the undertaker and can't get Mama put away."

"Becky was Buster's own double-second cousin." The old man pops up like a rotten egg in water. "If he hain't got no more principle about him . . ."

Buck butts in. "You got a bone to pick with him, Old Man, go pick it!"

"I hain't hankering to see his yeller face!"

"He ain't fixing to up and offer," says Buck, right in the old man's face, "you know that!"

"You gotta go begging sometimes, Old Man." Pee Wee socks the front door with his fist.

"I hain't going begging Buster for nothing," the old man says.

"Ain't Buster you gotta look to," Buck hoots. "It's the county."

"Same thang." The old man sets back, sulling again.

Pee Wee's sweating now, and I got a notion he's fixing to start in on me about keeping the house too hot. Shore nuf, in a minute he snatches the door open and the stiff wind whips at the new picture calendar over the head of the bed. A *bik bik bik* sound. A peaceful Jesus is kneeling in the garden above February 1960.

The old man shoots forward. "Shet that door, boy!"

"Well, you gone have to open it if you bring her home like she is." Pee Wee slams the door and hugs hisself, walking. "Undertaker's got her in a cold storage now. I'll be a S.B.!"

"You cussing your own dead mommer, boy!" The old man punches the air with his scrawny arm cocked. Generally, he'll let the boys say S.B. or G.D., but that's about it, because one time he knowed a man got struck down by lightning for cussing God under a pine tree.

Pee Wee's warming at the stove with his legs spraddled. Directly, he slacks off and the room gets still, and I listen to the leftover *bik bik bik* of Jesus over my head. When it stops, the lid on the bean pot picks up with the same racket.

"You so all-fired proud, Old Man!" Buck grits his teeth, sounds like he's trying to take the sore throat. He squats at the old man's knees like he's worshiping him. "You got a extra pension check laying around somewheres, huh?"

The old man turns his face to the wall and says it again: "Me and your mommer's done with one another, y'all do what you want to about hit."

"I see old Loujean there's just setting taking it easy," Earl says, doing his dead level best to change the subject. He ain't dumb as he looks.

The baby cries.

Buck

Soon as we get done with dinner, I set out on foot for Buster's, leaving pore lil ole Loujean with the baby bawling and the old man blabbing. Generally, you'll find Buster propped up at the courthouse across the way, or at Hoot's store, south of the crossing, or out scouting for somebody to hoodoo. But you can count on him to be eating and sleeping at his house.

To make the old man think I left in the post truck, I give Pee Wee the keys—and him in the shape he's in!—and watch him back it out of the grass alley between our place and the post office, then turn off 94, heading south on 129 for the Florida line. Me done wishing I'd let Earl do the driving, but one of them's about as dependable as the other. You could put them in a paper sack, shake it up, and dump it, and they'd all fall out about the same time.

I decide to wait a minute before crossing the hardroad, see if the old man comes out the side door in the alley, or maybe around the front of the old white-board store where we live in the back. Three little rooms overlooking Troublesome Creek. Owned by Buster, of course. Through the finger-smudged dust on the plate-glass windows, I can see clean to the other side of the store, where if the old man's coming out our front door, he'll show in a minute around the corner. Buster's using the front part for a packhouse now: old cocoaler crates, nail kegs, laying mash, and a bunch of junk he cheated somebody out of on a debt—a couple of truck batteries, some greasy tools, slat side bodies off some poor soul's truck, a dozen rolled-up cotton mattresses he claimed after old man Keel died at the mattress factory on the river. Even the weighing scales off Rufus's fish truck.

When Buster went to buying up places to rent out, and getting into bigger doings, he rented out the store in two parts, front and back. They's been a café here, and then a whorehouse, even a picture show, with Buster dabbling in all of them from the county commissioner's office across the road. I look any day for him to tear the old building down and put up a filling station, being on the corner of two major highways like it is. He's been making hisself too scarce here lately, not dunning us every breath for the rent and trying to scare the mess out of me.

Well, looks like the old man ain't coming; he'd have to get up and out to do that, and he's feeling too sorry for hisself right now. That's how he gets around beating the bushes for money when we get in a tight. But you can't never tell where he might turn up, bad as he is to plunder. Steer clear of the dumpsters and generally you got it made.

I hurry on out of the grass alley, already in half shadow, and cross the hardroad, in full sun, looking both ways. Everybody in Cornerville's likely still eating dinner, but the light at the crossing goes from red to green to yellow, just like traffic's lined up and waiting. Nobody don't pay it no attention nohow; that's just some more of Buster's doings, trying to put Swanoochee County on the map.

Much as I need to be in the post woods, working, I have to get this business about Mama straightened out before Monday, so I can get on back to work. Uncle Sam and the lectric company don't shut the doors cause somebody's mama dies. If I had my druthers, I'd pay the undertaker out of my own pocket, but we've had a rainy spell and can't hardly get in the post woods for bogging down. Fence posts ain't bringing but fifty cent apiece. Course if I had good help, I could make a living at it. Pee Wee's laid up drunk about half the time, Alamand's gone sorry away from daydreaming, and Earl . . . far as I'm concerned, he can go on back to Tarver and lay up at his mama's.

But other businesses I been in ain't brung in no better cash. Me and the old man used to take the boys and put up outhouses all over the county: sheds, barns, johns, packhouses, you name it. We didn't never one time come out on it. Everybody wanted something for nothing. Like Judge Crews. We went over there early one hot summer morning to put him up a one-hole john and stayed on two whole days, working from can to can't. He kept coming up with idears to get more out of us than we'd bargained on. All we was belonged to do was build him a plain john; before we got done, he had us putting four holes in a one-seat bench, diamond-cut, plus a wall of shelfs for seeds and tools. We lost bad on that one, and the old man got disheartened. That's when he quit working. For a while there, he tinkered around on Buster's trucks and tractors, but he weren't no hand to mechanic. Then they had a bad falling-out when Buster set his sights on becoming a county commissioner so he could get holt of the money my great-uncle John left to the county.

Before that, Buster and the old man was buddy-buddy, one of them drawing from the county about as much as the other—pension for pension, doctor doings, funerals, dirt hauled in for a ramp—like a big trust fund set up by Great-Uncle John, who is still talked about in these parts as "Big John," which had to do with that big black felt hat brung by train from New York to Fargo, along with a pair of real leather boots, which he wore when he come in from the flatwoods that morning during the Depression to bestow on the county what it needed to keep going. That money was the county's anyhow cause of the taxes due them on Great-Uncle John's bootleg whiskey business. Not that ery one of them (the county) said nothing, they just played like he was giving them a gift—and wadn't that dandy!— all of them knowing it was a debt being repaid, even to the last when Big John up and died and left it all to the county—gift/debt—and by then it wadn't all that necessary since The War had put us back on our feet. So Buster took the surplus.

And that's about the gist of it: the grudges and begrudging feeding down from that legacy till nobody under fifty can't hardly recollect where it all started, or figger yet how it might one of these days stop, but that it is, it just *is,* the grudges and begrudging as always starting from something so earthshaking nobody can't forget and linking to those uncommon, downtrodden, overblown predicaments that us Scurvys for all time have fell heir to and always will. A Scurvy don't just die—even living to a hundred or better—they die somehow that stays with you (like Aunt Becky done, about five years ago) but won't fit in writing on a tombstone; it would take too many words and wouldn't read real nohow. But we don't never quit telling it. When we have a falling-out, it's the same way, outlandish and lasting.

I come by it honest—me and Buster ain't got no use for one another neither. A few years back, he commissioned me to haul a load of shine for him, and I didn't come out atall. I just plain don't have the nerve for it. At least hauling fence posts, I don't have to dodge the law and put up with Buster's mess.

Weak in the knees, I cross the courtyard with its thready dead grass and then the hardroad back of the courthouse, heading up the school-bus shortcut where the brittle, gray, two-story hotel sets on the corner amongst liveoaks older than ery Scurvy. The sun on the asphalt smells tarry and sharp and pitches my shadow ahead where I can see the old brick schoolhouse roof, black against the blue sky, at the end of the road. Low smoke drifts from a pile of burning leaves, across from the schoolhouse, left side of the road, where Buster's backyard hooks to another yard, rake marks up to the chinaberry tree which serves as a divider between one plot of dirt and the other, both Buster's.

Cutting cross his backyard, I notice Aunt Ida Mae's put out a washing on the clothesline between the chinaberry tree and the low white house. Bleached white towels flap in the wind loaded with the dry click of crickets and burning leaves and the flat tallowy smell of stewing beef. It's now that I miss Mama, and I can't afford to. I got to keep my mind on business and my eyes on Buster. At the back door, a flock of plump Rhode Island Reds is pecking at a scatter of collard stems. When they see me, they go crazy, fluff up their feathers and squawk like I'm after them. Their fuss don't do nothing for my nerves; not that I'm scared of Buster, I just dread having to beg. And him of all people! That's the old man's place to do that, in my estimation, but I reckon he's got his own reasons for despising Buster. Most folks around Cornerville do; but most folks don't show it, in case they need Buster. A county commissoner can come in handy or he can do you some dirt. Buster's got more power than the Georgia gov'nor.

"Aunt Ida Mae?" I call, knocking on the screen door and flapping it in its frame.

I can hear her framming around in her kitchen and swearing. She swears at me, before she sees who it is, and I don't take it personal. That's just Aunt Ida Mae for you, and I know everybody she swears at is her husband, Buster.

"Come on in," she hollers out in her muffled voice.

I don't. I'm here on business this time, and Buster handles business under the chinaberry tree. Besides, I ain't been by since me and Buster had our run-in a few years back. So much time's passed now I'd be ashamed to just walk in like I used to. Used to, I'd be running in and out, slamming doors with the rest of Aunt Ida Mae's younguns (she's got two sets, one about my age, and a new drove of littluns). I just found out I'm a man, and I wish I hadn't. I swallow hard.

She comes walking heavy-footed, kicks the screen door open, and ducks out, spitting a brown string of snuff juice off the doorsteps where I'm standing next to Buster's little turned-up-toed brogans. The chickens cluck and scatter, then gather again, pecking at the slick brown streak as it dulls and dries in on the powdery dirt.

"Shoo!" she says, waving her hands. "Git on away from here, you rascals!" Her squinched brown eyes settle on me while she fusses at the chickens. She wipes her shirred mouth on the hem of her white apron. Wouldn't smile for nothing, don't never mince words.

"I heared about Louella," she says. "When y'all looking to bury her?"

"Sunday," I say, like we done made all the arrangements.

"I'll be there," she says—a real kindness on her part. If she ever leaves the house, except to set on the porch with her sister Cordy across the road, I don't know of it. "Tell Loujean I'm cooking a little something to send over," she adds.

Nothing sweet in what she says, just earnest. I prechate that.

"I reckon you here to see Buster?" she says. Another real kindness on her part, since for the life of me I can't get the words out. She's my mama's own double-second cousin and the spitting image, except Mama was a little grayer and woreout from doing without and having babies by herself. The last two died, before this one she had the other night, and she mourned them like a cow would a calf: doing her best to rouse them, bellering awhile, then going on about her business, looking out for the bull. (Dumpsters ain't the onliest place you got to dodge to keep from happening up on the old man.)

Buster pops into view behind the screen door in his white socks, short knotty arms crooked. He snatches his coat off the back of a chair and tugs it on. Looks like he's in a deep study. One of Aunt Ida Mae's younguns starts squalling at the other end of the house, and she takes off at a half-run. Coming out the door, Buster nearly bout knocks me off the doorsteps, then drops right down beside his brogans and starts knocking the sand out of one and then the other—makes like he don't know I'm on the place—and pulls them on, yanking the shoestrings tight. His close-set green eyes fret over the bows he's making, like he don't want to chance making a bad impression.

He looks strange making bows. Under his blue shirt, his hard belly is strutted. He looks like a big man that's shrunk. If you was to see him off just standing around, and didn't know who he was, you wouldn't think he was nobody. "You here for a favor, Scooter?" he asks and trots off the doorsteps.

He says it so fast that I have to think a minute, then my blood goes to boiling.

He's under the chinaberry tree now, standing with his stumpy legs spraddled, trying to light a cigarette. Every match he strikes the wind blows out—one, two, three. Then looks like he's fixing to do some magic trick; he strikes another match and cups his hands quick, and cigarette smoke flows through his fingers and curdles into the leaf smoke, and he could be the devil hisself wading through the sulfur fires of hell.

I light up a cigarette too and go over, standing off a piece where the circle of shade meets the sun. I can hear Aunt Ida Mae fussing with the younguns inside the house;

next thing you know, she'll be setting nussing them. My mama made over.

"I come to see if I could get some help from the county to put Mama away," I say.

"Don't do that no more." Buster takes a hard pull on his cigarette, then thumps it to Aunt Ida Mae's collard patch. "Law come down on us." He's putting on a Chapstick now, with his rind lips pooched. "Right after old man Keel died at the mattress factory," he adds. He gazes down at the cigarette butts strowed under the tree with dingy splatters of chicken mess. (Aunt Ida Mae don't rake up under the tree, just around it; that's how much she thinks of Buster and his doings.)

My hands is shaking like the shadows of the chinaberry leaves on the dirt. I'm stopped up and feel like I'm taking the flu. The wind changes and the smoke from the leaf pile rolls away from us.

"Say the post business ain't doing so hot, huh?" Buster shifts feet and lays into the tree trunk.

"I'm making out," I say and have to take a draw on my cigarette to keep from adding "without you." Let me get Mama buried good, and they ain't no tellings what I'll say to him.

"I hear you!" he says. He always plays games when he's making a trade, and putting up with his way of warming up is part of it.

"It's been rainy here lately," I say.

"I hear you."

His head tapers from the temples up, like it's been squeezed in a vice; his wet-blond hair is combed straight back so it'll stand up and make him look taller. He speaks:

"Yeah, Louella was as fine a woman as they is in this county."

That's part of it too, how he hemhaws around before he takes off and leaves you hanging. "We got to come up with a couple hundred before the undertaker'll put her away," I say.

"Yeah, as fine a woman as I knowed of . . ." he says, by hisself now, listening to some racket from the yard of the hotel up the road a piece.

"I don't reckon you could see your way clear to let me borry a little off you till I can get on my feet."

He acts like he don't hear me, straggles off toward the road, and stands a minute, looking toward the courthouse. He's got deep pockets in his navy blue britches, and his hands is sunk to the wrist, fingering keys and pocket change. Looks like he's fixing to hand me a nickel and tell me to go on. "Me and you's done business before, Scooter," he says, turning quick and bearing down on me with that mixed look of little-man mischief and toughened snake.

"I meant from the county money," I say and mash out my cigarette with the toe of my boot.

"Same thing; don't mess with that no more," he says. "You innerstid in running a little shine again?" He palms the smoky air. "That is, providing I can put some confidence in you this time?"

"Don't mess with that no more," I say and walk around him.

"Being as how we're close kin," he says, "I'm willing to look over how you run out on me last time."

"I'll mull it over," I say and keep walking.

"You could of ended up a rich man, Scooter," he hollers after me.

Or a dead one, I think. I don't have nothing will do to say to him right now, so I keep going. But I know I'll be back. He does too.

Old Man

Them boys can't pull nothing over on me, Buster neither.

I sneak on around to the yonder side of the hotel dumpster and duck down behind hit for Buck to go by. He can't see me for looking. Gazes square at the dumpster, then mopes on off up the road like a man toting fifty pound of block-ice on his shoulders.

I'm so mad I could whip him in front of everybody in Cornerville. Right out in the open. Would, if hit weren't for Louella laying a corpse. Going to Buster, first off! Hain't tried nothing else.

I pick up a stick and go to scratching in the rain-pecked dirt, still squatting and keeping a bead on Buster, now circling in the road like a buzzard and watching Buck till he gets to the courthouse and turns along the sidewalk beside 129.

In a minute, Buster takes off walking, whistling up the hardroad in Buck's tracks. I let him get good and past, then raise up slow, and he quits whistling and cackles out but don't never look back. He's seen me.

"You lowdown, white-headed S.B.!" I holler and chunk my stick at him. "Don't look like no Scurvy to me."

He keeps walking with his head high.

They's a beer bottle poking up from a paper sack of trash in the dumpster. I could chunk that too, or maybe that piece of scrap iron laying to one side. But I don't since I figger I might need him; shore as my name is Lay Scurvy, I'm gone be needing him before this thing with Louella is over.

Buster's out of range now, stepping high over the courtyard railing and heading for the back door of the courthouse.

I hain't getting into hit. I go on about my business.

Somebody's throwed out a right good lady's shoe, a black high-heel with a twisted toe. I dig hit out and twist hit straight, then scratch around in the dumpster for the mate. I can't come up with hit. Well, maybe Sonia Lee can wear hit with one of her other shoes.

All I got to do is think about that gal and . . . Great God! I'll hold on to the shoe till Louella's put away; wouldn't be fitting to go sparking till after the funeral. Come Monday, things oughta be back to normal. Till then, I gotta go set around the house, make hit clear to them boys they can't dump this thing with Louella in my lap.

But I got a feeling I'm gone end up with Buster under yonder chinaberry tree.

Loujean

The baby cries the whole time I'm washing the dinner dishes. I feel like crying with her, but she's crying enough for the both of us. I try to think what Mama would do, so I set down in the old man's chair by the door, rocking and singing: "Rock of ages, cleft for me, Let me hide myself in thee. . . ."

She don't no more care than nothing where I'm singing or not, but the racket the both of us is making will have Miss Cleta from the post office back over here any minute. I stop singing and say, "Shh, now," and try to feed the baby some more formula from her suck bottle. Her mouth is a round red hole; the nipple goes straight in, and I can see white drops of milk on her lizard tongue, fixing to strangle her. I take it out and hold her up, staring at her teensy bright face. She keeps bawling. I ain't been one hour fed her anyhow.

"Little baby," I say, "if you don't hush up, they gone think I can't look out for you."

I don't say what's next, not out loud, since saying stuff sometimes makes it happen. But deep down I feel a burning, thinking about her going to the county.

Here I am, hoping to get something from the county, and hoping the county don't take nothing from me.

"Maybe it's too hot in here." I don't feel nowhere near as solid as I sound. I get up and open the front door.

I stand in the doorway, bouncing the baby on my shoulder, her still bawling. I make sure the cold don't get to her ears by tucking the blanket about her smooth, round head.

The wind's died down for the evening. By dark, it'll likely pick up again. I wait there in the cold going sun and gaze out over 129 at the bony bare sweetgums along the creek banks. I can't see the black stream twining through the woods, but I know if the water there right now ain't gone to running backards, like everything else, it'll soon make its way past the cemetery to the Alapaha River.

"Poor lil ole baby," I say. "Poor Mama." I feel myself primping up to cry and think it won't do. School buses line up at the red light, squawking brakes, and three of them turn north on 129, dipping at the creek. Brighter yellow than the swole sun, and them loaded with younguns, they pass right by me. I wave and a couple of white hands lift like doves.

I do love school. Give the chance, I could outread and outfigger ery one in my class. That's what my teachers always say. That's all right; I'd of quit sooner or later anyhow.

I cry a little bit, standing there in the door, smelling the burnt diesel off the buses. I cry for myself and for Mama, for the baby and with the baby. I cry for Mama suffering with uremic poisoning night before last. I don't cry for her the way she is now, asleep in Jesus. I cry for the baby since the Bible says to weep over them coming into the world and rejoice over them going out. I wish I could really feel that, but I'm ascared my crying's for the wrong reasons really, switched around.

I shut the door and stand, cold with the sun on the other side.

Earl

— — — — — — — — — —Pee Wee left the post
truck parked along 129, at the Georgia-Florida line, then
went on in the cement-block beer joint called The Line.
So close to the hardroad we can feel the wind off the
transfer trucks when they pass. *Whoom shoosh* about every
ten minutes for the past two hours. Me and Alamand just
setting in the truck, him with his eyes on the white road
ahead, Florida side, and me with my eyes on the blacktop
in the rearview mirror, Georgia side. Tunnel of tall pines
now shuttering the cold low sun.

I scoot over under the steering wheel, crank up, and
back the truck between two souped-up pickups, then head
north up the blacktop straightaway.

"Where we going?" Alamand shifts his boots on the
rusted-out floorboard, where cold and gas fumes shoot
through a crack.

"Going back up there to Mr. R. D.'s," I say.

"Shoot!" says Alamand. "Rich man like that ain't gone
let you have no money."

"Ain't looking for no handout," I say loud above the

roar and rattle of the truck, "and Mr. R. D. ain't hardly no rich man, just hardworking."

"What about Pee Wee?" Alamand says, settling in for the ride.

"We coming right on back." I can tell Alamand don't want to mess up his make-believing by hooking up with somebody real, but it's gone take somebody real to come up with the money, else Loujean's gone be heartbroke.

I come in a wan of hocking my Old Timer this morning in Jasper, to get that pot of white plastic Easter lilies at the dimestore for Loujean's mama (that was before Buck and them got turned down by the undertaker). Chickened out's what I done, cause you never know when some tough-talking joker's gone jump on you for looking dumb, and I'd about as soon part with Loujean as my pocketknife. Got me a dollar in my pocket and about fifty owing to me, and white lilies ain't gone cut it with Loujean.

When we turn down the dirt lane to Mr. R. D.'s, I see him sawing logs in the woodpile in front of his house. Lil ole new house he just built, painted white. Set out pine saplings all around it in neat rows running to the highway. Gray smoke's feathering from the heater pipe stuck through the new tin top where the setting sun torches it gold.

I pull in behind a blue truck loaded with pulpwood and start to get out and Alamand says, "Guess I'll just set here till you get back."

I close the door and mosey on over to the woodpile where Mr. R. D.'s chainsaw is spitting orange sawdust and white smoke and growling like a mad bear. He sees me and nods and I pick up his axe and go to splitting pine blocks into heater-size firewood. Smells of cold pine tar, oak smoke, frying ham, and sweat. His green shirt's glued to his blocky back, his thick neck is red, them pulpwood arms working up and down on the chainsaw like he ain't doing nothing but pumping water.

About a half-dozen blond-headed younguns skip off the low front porch and go to chasing one another through the pines. Two spotted bird-dog pups yipping behind them. Everlast one of them's wearing shoes.

Directly, Mr. R. D. idles the saw and sets it on a block, then chokes it, and I can still hear it growling and grinding when it stops. He turns around and tips his cap bill up so I can see his sober brown eyes. "How you, Earl?" he says.

"Awright," I say. "How you, Mr. R. D.?"

"Can't complain," he says and wipes his broad forehead with his right arm. Sawdust and freckles on bunched muscles. "You here looking for work?"

"No sir," I say, "I'm still helping Buck and them haul fence posts. I just . . ."

He butts in: "They a bunch of go-getters, them Scurvy boys, ain't they?" He laughs and looks over at the beat-up old post truck. Alamand's white face in the side window is still as a picture.

I guess Mr. R. D. means me too; I used to help him cut and haul pulpwood before I took up with Buck and them serious. Bent on courting Loujean, much as anything. Now ain't no way of asking her to marry me till I can make a honest living, and courting her's keeping me from making a honest living. And ain't no way I'd leave Buck and them in such a fix. Mr. R. D. goes to stacking firewood in his arms, chin-high, and calls to the younguns to come get in the splinters. They come running, them and the pups, dodging through the pines. Not a wormy one in the litter.

I gather me a big turning of firewood too and trail in behind Mr. R. D. to the back of the house. Over the wire fence, white shoats root in the gray dirt, and red pole cows graze green shoots in the burned-off pasture. Sun wallowing behind tall, bristly pines along the riverbanks.

"Mr. R. D.," I say, catching up to him at the back doorsteps. He bumps open the white door and steps inside and drops the wood by the fat black heater, a loud calamity, about the time I'm getting set to ask him for the money—just enough to pay down on Loujean's mama's funeral—and I don't know if I was gone ask him in the first place, and I don't know why not, but I have a feeling it's cause asking some low-principled loafer like myself would make a whole lot more sense. But ain't no low-principled loafer like myself gone have no money.

In the yellow kitchen, Mr. R. D.'s wife, Sallie Lou, is standing over the cookstove, frying ham in a black iron pan. Wearing what looks like one of Mr. R. D.'s blue-striped shirts. She sees me and says, "Well, if it ain't Earl," and smiles and pushes her dark hair from her little pointy face. Expecting again. "You younguns run wash up for supper," she says to the drove filing in behind me, and slides a waiter full of puffy, brown biscuits from the oven. Then to me, "Ain't that Alamand out there in the truck?" I tell her it is Alamand in the truck, and she goes bounding barefoot through the house to the front door. Swole belly covered by her man's shirt.

Don't look nothing like Loujean, but she reminds me of Loujean, of the kind of life I want to make for Loujean, what I want to do with Loujean. I want to sleep with her at night, and sometimes maybe even in the daytime. I want to eat with her after work in a kitchen just like this kitchen, and I want to be tough and tender like Mr. R. D., so when some low-principled loafer like me comes begging for what I've come by honest, I can shame him into leaving us alone in our yellow kitchen, in our white house, in our bed I can't picture except in my head. Me and Loujean making babies.

"Hey, Alamand," Miss Sallie Lou yells out the door. He don't even look at her. "Alamand, hey," she yells between her hands, "get on out and come eat."

He gets out of the truck grinning and comes tripping toward the house, one boot toe snagging on the stitching-together grass. Before he gets through the door, he's got younguns hanging all over him. Ain't a youngun around don't love Alamand, I guess cause they know he's one of them.

Wellsir, we wind up sticking our feet under Miss Sallie Lou's table, eating her biscuits and cane syrup and fried ham till we're bout to bust, then listening to Mr. R. D.'s war stories, to repay him, till out in the night, and I don't never once tell him about Loujean's mama dying nor ask him for a dime, just end up leaving my last dollar on his eating table to prove I can pay my own way.

PART TWO

PART TWO

Alamand

_ _ _ _ _ _ _ _ _ Same blue-grass playing on the jukebox again, wrapping up with fiddles gone wild.

Then it stops. But Miss Annette goes on, making her rounds, putting out the salt and pepper shakers. When she gets to my table she smiles.

"You still the best cook in the county," I say.

And she says, "The onliest one too," walking off with her eyes rolling. But I can tell my bragging gets away with her, the way she switches off in that white waitressing dress with one hand up, limp at the wrist. Her fingernails is bit to the quick. She's good to me—ain't never let me pay for my eats. I wonder if she's sorry for me, or maybe looking for something back. Naw, she's old enough to be my mama.

I always try to show a interest in her, since she come from someplace else. Not many people comes here to live cause they want to. Specially not no divorced women. Her kind's as scarce as mine. She don't give them no call to, but every man in these parts thinks he can go with her since she's divorced. I can picture her leaving some fat, sloppy drunk and coming here to open the old café for some peace and quiet.

She's got purple dot scars on her face from where she used to have pimples, and sometimes when my face breaks out, I catch her looking like she's sorry for me, and I don't even worry about stuff like that.

She's just gone around to the back of the jukebox and put it on free and punched in my song again. She knows it's my favorite—and I been knowed to dream up stuff too. Pro'bly she just likes it her ownself, but what if she wants me to play up to her and I don't? She did say how sorry she was about Mama when I first come in. Then she made me breakfast and punched in three blue-grass tunes in a row. I love blue-grass cause it's frolicsome and happy and I'm not. I act like I am though.

I'm figgering how to get up in the middle of the song and just walk out, but what if she's punched in another one for me? All I want right now is to go someplace and set by myself. Maybe find me a sheet of paper and draw. A old piece of pasteboard or some Sheetrock will do. Don't make no difference, long as it'll draw.

On Saturdays, off from the post woods or school, I used to set at the house and read comic books till two in the evening to keep from dwelling on my drawing. But when I turned fourteen, I made up my mind to get on out so nobody wouldn't think nothing was wrong with me. If I drawed at home, they thought it for sure. Always bugging me, all except Loujean. After Aunt Becky died, I took to going to her lil ole house—a quiet spot, set off to itself behind the quarters—where I could draw the livelong day and not hear nothing but younguns playing in the quarters, maybe some doves crying off in the woods. Locusts humming, a nothing sound. Sometimes one cricket by hisself sounds like a squeaky door.

Aunt Becky knowed about it, too. And sometimes, while she was still a-living, she'd preach to me about a idle mind and all, but she'd stick my drawings up on her walls to look at. And every once in a while, she'd ask me to come up with a flower or a tree, but I couldn't. I tried. I ain't never been able to draw somebody else's idears. Wish I could have for her though, after what-all they say she done for me, even if I don't have no memory of her saving me. The song's winding up again, and Miss Annette's watching me from her stool behind the counter. Generally, she goes on about her business, nice to me but not the kind of nice that means something. I smile and wait while the hook arm of the jukebox jitters the record to its slot. The jukebox clicks and hums. I suck in. The hum dies and the rainbow lights dim like the jukebox is waiting too.

I get up slow, to show I ain't in no rush, and take my plate to the counter. Nothing but a yellow smear where I sopped my biscuit in the egg. "Them's some good-eating biscuits," I say.

She keeps smiling—not flirty, just kind of timid, or like she's not too won over by me nor nobody else. Her red mouth turns down like she's sad. I hope it's not to do with me always trying to eat free.

"Let me pay you," I say, reaching in my empty right pocket.

"On the house," she says.

"Naw," I say, digging and gazing off.

"One of these days I'll get you to paint a picture of a hamburger on that window there." She nods toward the front wall of hazy glass where fake ferns hang against CAFÉ painted backward: ÉFAC.

I can feel the blood in my face, like hot thorns sticking. I can't picture painting no hamburger, how it would look if I done it, but I can picture how she'd want it—a straight hamburger. I could do a hamburger maybe if a cartoon character was chomping down on it. I start to tell her that, but I don't since I can't never be sure how a picture will come out till it's done. She wouldn't no more understand that than Aunt Becky did about the rose I drawed her. Loujean's the onliest one will set and wait till I get done and then take a picture for what it is. Buck, he'll say I oughta send some off to the funny papers. Make some money off them, he says, I've heard tell of people got rich doing that. They wouldn't have no use for them, the funny papers wouldn't. I'm not that good; besides, I just like making up stuff. But Buck says, If you ain't making nothing—meaning money—quit.

"Prechate it," I say to Miss Annette and fish a toothpick from the shot glass by the cash register. I fix the round stools in a perfect row for her, hoping she'll forget about the hamburger picture, then head out.

"Alamand," she calls after me—I've done made it to the door, got my hand on the knob—"tell Loujean if she needs any help with the baby to let me know."

I suck in, let go, and pat my stomach. "I'll tell her and we prechate it. Looks like she's holding up pretty good." What I meant was, she's handling it pretty good.

Miss Annette just smiles, maybe tickled at me. Maybe she's not thinking about me atall. Or maybe she's waiting for me to ask her to go to the back room where she lives. I ain't never been with but one woman, Sonia Lee, that lil ole crazy across Troublesome Creek that happened up here from Florida. And then I just did it since everybody else was—Buck, Pee Wee, and Earl. I ain't for shore Earl did, though. He went in her bedroom and come right on back out, grinning and shaking his head like she didn't suit his taste. Sweet on Loujean's what he is.

Once Earl saved my life—maybe twice. But that one time, in particular, he like to killed me trying to save me. Now that's the kind of thing I'd like to draw, if I could, if I had me a big enough piece of paper and had the time. If I could I'd draw us, me and Earl, just little fellows, him about a head taller than me, and us following Buck and Pee Wee off to go in swimming in the Alapaha River. They was bad to get into meanness, even back then; Mama couldn't never keep up with us. Shucks, once you got up about five, you was on your own. How could you draw that?

I could draw Buck and Pee Wee swimming out across the river, where it runs deep and black up under the bridge, and me and Earl wading across downstream where the water is shallow and clear, sparkling like the sun is buried under the scalloped white sand (white chalk from the schoolhouse might work for the sand). Buck and Pee

Wee could be coming out on the other bank where the cement bridge posts have red writing—bunch of boys got holt of some spray paint's what it was. But one thing I can't lay hands on is no paint. Anyhow, Buck and Pee Wee could be climbing up the banks, thick with tupelos and willows, and take out running for Buster's broomsage patch (I'd have to draw two pictures, I guess, to tell this story).

Earl would hike up his wet holey dungarees and then take off, gaining on them (how to draw action?) and leave me straggling behind. Him loping like a yearling deer through the head-high broomsage that lays over like it will in the wind. It is sunny-smelling and silky (can't draw smells), tickles my face and chest (can't draw feeling, can't draw the dirt cool where the broomsage hills grow thick at the roots, or the heat of the sun bearing down on my wet head, blistering my scalp; can't draw hearing them fade out toward the woods, but can draw the green pines stitching the blond broomsage to the blue sky). No paint.

I might can't draw this whole thing atall; but then again I might figger out how to do what no other artist in the world has ever done before. I might be great: Alamand the artist.

In what I'd draw as the middle of the broomsage patch, I'd have me chewing on a straw and listening to them whooping, coming back, three heads bobbing above the level blond broomsage (no, hazel, the color of Buck's eyes). They would circle round me, closing in, and Buck and Pee Wee would tussle me to the ground, then drag me to a old fence post sticking up above the broomsage. Earl looking on, but not helping, as they lift me high to the sun-bleached sky and set me on top of that post, then take off again, whooping like Injuns. All of them.

Earl ain't no bigger than a minute, but tough as a gator. Buck and them have done give up trying to kill him since he won't cry nor nothing. Don't never tattle.

I'm bad blistered, in the picture, all of us are from going without shirts. Me, in just my underdrawers. My back and chest and shoulders burning up, stinging like I've got in a wast nest. My backend throbs from where the top of the post is jobbing in me. I pee on myself, feel it run off hot down my legs, down the fence post, my arms straight out for balance, like a scarecrow's. I cry, I can't stop. I don't know how long I set there: hours ain't hours no more but whole days, seems like. Too scared of falling off that post to move, looking out at the heat above the broomsage, runny as old window glass, at the blue sky melting down behind the tops of the trees. Tight hum of locusts ringing in my ears. If I close my eyes, I'll tumble off.

I don't expect them right on back. I just cry and watch the sun crossing the sky, east to west, my shadow switching sides. I've licked my lips till they sting, a circle of red I can see without looking. I ain't never been no thirstier. My shoulders and back is aching from where I've stiffened up to stay put: a-scared of falling off, a-scared of staying on. Too tired to cry, too miserable to quit. I can see to the end of the world, a brown blur, green where it drops off, where night will come creeping like a panther. I feel growed to that post.

Long about sundown, I see one brown head bobbing through the broomsage patch, coming for me. I know it's Earl before he gets there. "I come back after you, little bubber," he hollers out, still a good piece off, and running like he hadn't stopped since he left.

I'm whining like a hurt dog.

"Jump on down," he says, standing up under me, hassling (I got it, I got it, I got it! I'll draw balloons up over my characters' heads with what they're saying printed inside). I jump. The seat of my underdrawers snags on the top of the post and cuts into my straddle—I won't never make water no more. Splinters in my chapped behind, my back rubbing raw where I'm hung from the post like a coon hide to dry. The elastic of my drawers saws into my armpits.

Earl grabs my legs and yanks down and I let out a holler. He stands a minute, squinting up at my cooked face, his milky blue eyes tearing good now. He shines his top teeth, and I think he's fixing to bite me. I can't move nohow, can't hurt no worse. Then he goes to digging in his pocket for a old knife his daddy give him—says he's been sharpening it regular for just such emergency—and sets into sawing on one leg of my drawers, gashing up my side like hog fat for cracklings.

I drop on top of him with one foot still hooked in my snagged drawers. And then nothing won't do him but to jerk the splinters out. "I prechate it," I say (printed inside a balloon, of course), "but I was better off on top of that fence post."

Hell, I didn't even say that, and ain't nothing new

about drawing balloons over heads with writing in them; funny papers is been using that trick for a hundred years, which is about how long it would take to come up with a way to draw this story, and even if I could draw it and broke in Hoot Walters's store and stole that whole roll of white freezer paper, the picture wouldn't fit.

Buck

Being as how me and Earl wadn't making no headway in the post woods by ourself, I give it up and start on back to the house. Saturdays, you can look for Alamand and Pee Wee to nigger off—woods is too wet anyhow—and Earl . . . I can't turn around without that rascal up under me, driving me crazy with them long tales. If he's trying to take my mind off my troubles, he's getting a fooling.

On the road home from the woods near Needmore, I look over at him flapping his gums and setting high in his brown-plaid shirt. You don't have to be smart to figger he is just as happy to be knocking off, though generally he'll work till he falls out. Don't have to pay him if you don't want to, that's how crazy he is—No sir, if you ain't got it this week, don't worry about it.

Robins is pecking along the frosty shoulders of the hardroad, flocking up as the truck gets to them, then lighting in the gallberry borders of the pinewoods. So I'm looking for a robin story out of Earl. Shore nuf: "I tell you, when I was coming up, I was glad to see wintertime," he says. "Soon as them robins made it down here from Upnorth, gobbling on them gallberries, I'd set out and shoot 'em. Sold 'em for a nickel apiece in the quarters." He acts like he's fifty years old, stead of seventeen, jawing about old times.

"You done told me," I say. You can't insult Earl for nothing.

"If I was you," he says, "I'd pull off the road here and shoot me a mess with that .22 there." He eyes my rifle propped between us. "Yessir, like I always say, ain't nothing like a good mess of robins and rice and it wintertime." When he gets like this, you bout as well let him get it out of his system or you'll be listening to his long stories all day. I ain't in no mood. I let the window down and chunk out my cigarette butt and pull off on the shoulder. Ditches is level with still, black water, like icebox tea with a skim of ice.

"Take it and get on out of here," I say, shoving the rifle at him.

He jerks it up, grinning, and eases out, tipping around the back of the truck with my .22 aimed at the gallberry bushes across the ditch. I set here, waiting, knowing what I have to do about that business with Mama.

I must of waited on him thirty minutes while he drag-assed around. He picked off robins, three in a row, then gathered them up, grinning back at me, and set off wandering along the dead-grass ditches to check for signs of pike in the water. The grass along the edges is turning from brown to yellow where the sun's coming up over the pines and thawing the frost and ice.

I don't have all day. I crank up the truck and set down

on the horn. He jumps, then heads up the ditch to the other side of the truck, flopping the robins through the window to the floorboard. He gets in and props the .22 between us, still grinning.

When I start to pull out, the truck wheels go to spinning, then sink to the hubs in a hole.

"Let up and ease out," he says, hanging his head out the window.

I hit it then, and mud slings everywhere. He looks back at me with specks of mud like moles all over his face.

"Get out and shove a couple of pine slabs up under the tires," I say.

He gets out and plunders around in the woods clearing where pines lay crisscross on a bed of bark, picks up a couple of slabs, and heads back. The woods is getting lighter and the yellow stumps and skint saplings is shining like raw skin.

He pokes one of the slabs under the right rear tire and hollers, "Hit it!"

I mash down on the gas with the tires spinning, black mud flying from the hardroad to the ditch, then ease on out. In the mirror, I can see him backing off, black and slick as a mudcat. He goes to laughing and raking mud off his sleeves and pants, slinging his hands as he lopes down the ditch. He takes off his brown-plaid shirt and rolls it up, scrubbing his hairless white chest and shoulders with it, then kneels down, scooping that icy water to his face and arms.

Back in the truck, he drops his work shirt on the floorboard with the robins and takes his yellow Sunday shirt, folded neat between us, and pulls it on.

"I ain't got all day, Earl," I say.

He buttons it while I drive, him just a-grinning.

I done got sorry for him. Looks like he's plum satisfied to be putting up with us and us treating him like we're putting up with him. "You want to get out at your mama's?" I say when I get to the railroad crossing at Tarver. One low red house, set back from the tracks, with a black rooster on the frosty yard.

"If it's all the same with you," he says, "I'll ride on into Cornerville with you."

If I had time to mess around, truth is they ain't nobody I'd ruther mess around with than Earl. But I don't. I don't know if he's crazy or just good-hearted, but I do know he knows how to live. Nothing don't bother him. And when I get this business with Buster behind me, I'm gone see if I can't take up some of Earl's habits.

I light another cigarette, soon as we get in sight of Cornerville, driving on past the hip-roofed schoolhouse and houses set in rows along the sidewalk to the red light. I think again about how nobody don't pay that light no attention, but I reckon a red light at Christmastime makes a pretty decoration.

"I'll get out here," Earl says, stuffing in his shirttail and bailing out with his robins, heading for our house on the north corner.

You don't have to be smart to figger he's taking them robins to Loujean. What he don't know is she's a bird lover, and anybody kills one winds up on her blacklist. When I look to the left, changing gears and fixing to turn, I see Buster setting in his truck in front of the courthouse. I go to cramping all over, like I do after working out in the heat all day. I turn left, then pull up in front of his truck, watching his tapered face through the windshield. He's setting with his finger on his lips, waiting on me, I guess, or maybe somebody else he's fixing to hoodoo. I get out and walk on over to his side of the truck. Got a old camper top on the back for hauling labor, so he says. He hauls what he wants to—deer out of season, shine, whatever he takes a notion to haul. Law don't mess with him cause he is the law, badge or not.

"What you say, Buck?" he says, looking straight ahead and rubbing his top lip with his finger.

I know he is saying good morning, but I go on and take it for a question. "I'll do it," I say, "but I need to do it now."

"I hear you," he says—still don't look at me. "Meet me here at nine on the dot tonight. You and Pee Wee."

"Pee Wee ain't in no shape," I say.

"I hear you," he says, cranking up. "Bring him anyhow."

I strike out to my truck, feeling like I've just sold my sister.

Loujean

I ain't out of the bed good before here comes Earl, knocking on the front door. The way he knocks twice is like somebody slipping around. Soft like that, I guess, to keep from waking up the baby, but he's been making eyes at me for so long, I wonder. Aggravating pest! Always picking his teeth with a broomstraw, popping my bra, yanking my hair, trying to come up with some smart saying. He's dumb! And now here he is fixing to wake up the baby.

The baby. I have to quit calling her that and name her something. Joyful Noise, I decide, Joy, for short; don't seem to mind no kind of racket. She'll sleep in spurts and then take spells of fretting between crying. I been up most of the night. The racket from the transfer trucks, pulling up and idling out front, is how come, that and worrying about the baby, not to mention Mama. How will we come up with the money to put her away?

At first, I figgered Buck would come up with something (I don't look for nothing out of the old man and the rest of them). Much as anything, I figgered the undertaker would come around and take it on good faith that we'll pay him on time. He sent a hearse right on to pick up Mama's body from the Jasper Hospital, where I was setting up with her when she died, so I was resting easy. I guess he didn't put two and two together till he took down Mama's name in writing and seen Scurvy on the end.

Now, here it is Saturday and nothing ain't been done. My heart is in a strut. I feel like her dying has just sunk in; and on top of that, looks like she'll stay in the funeral home till the Rapture.

While I go to the door, I wipe my eyes on my dresstail, standing a minute to pull myself together. I forgot to leave the spigots dripping last night, and the water pipes is froze up. I'll have to tote water from the courthouse. When I open the door, I spy the old man out pilfering in the dumpster across the road. I hate him. I know about him and Sonia Lee and I know he don't have it in him to feel no shame.

Earl is standing on the stoop, grinning, with three dead robins held by the feet. Their heads dangle like soggy knotted rags. Nussed up to his chest is a paper sack of groceries. "Loujean?" he says in a question. "I just come by to drop off some milk for the baby"—he holds out the poor little robins to me—"and a mess of robins for your dinner."

"Prechate it," I say, and make myself take the birds by their bony waxed toes.

He tiptoes on a-past me and sets the paper sack on the eating table, done crowded with tinfoil-covered dishes. The baby starts crying in the dresser drawer by the bed. Sounds like a little kitty meowing. "I done woke up the baby," he says.

"It's past time for her to be up," I say, dropping the dead robins by the woodstove and going to her. I bundle her up in her blanket and nuss her to me, smelling her moist fur head. While I change her diaper on the bed, Earl turns his head and whistles a tune to let me know he ain't looking. Then he goes over to the window and parts the curtains, reaches through the broke pane, and pulls in a piece of firewood. He opens the stove door latch with his boot toe and sticks the wood on the fire. Smoke boils out; he coughs and looks back at me.

"Reckon she'd catch cold if I was to open the door and let out the smoke?" he asks.

"Leave it alone," I say. "It'll clear up." I wish he would go. I'm getting used to being by myself with Joy. She's sweet and new, reminds me of a baby bird, but smells like spit-up. I know she's mine. I don't want her. She's like a case of head lice I just caught.

Thinking that, while her teensy legs pump, I nearly bout start crying again, have to think about them dead robins by the stove to keep from it. How hateful of Earl to of killed them. But deep down I know he didn't kill them out of hate. I start crying anyhow, me and the baby, hanging over her with one hand on each side pressing down on the mattress. She rolls left. Whatever happens to her is my fault. If she strangles, if she falls . . . I feel like God over people. I could make a tornado and blow her away. She rolls right and I let her. I don't want to be God. I cry harder.

I can't even hear myself crying, just her. My ears stop up, squeeze shut with my eyes. I don't care if Earl is here or not. I just don't care. I know what to do with a baby, and I don't mind work one bit. I just don't know what to do about Mama. I can picture her laying in that hospital bed, sweat popping out on her peaked face, her long gray hair unbound and matted. Moaning low so she won't scare me out of never having a baby of my own. She give me one. And I hate her for being so timid and letting the old man mess with her. It's all dirty. Just as well she left me a baby, since I won't never have one of my own now.

I pick up the baby and tote her over to the woodstove and set down in Mama's old nursing rocker. I don't look up at Earl; I can see his legs, his boots in front of the stove. Just standing there. He's holding out the suck bottle to me. I take it and poke the nipple in the baby's mouth, looking at her scrunched pink face. She cries a second and then sucks like a pig. I can hear my own stifled crying now. I cradle the baby to my heart and rock while I feed her. The clock is ticking on the mantelshelf, the only sound in the house except her sucking and my crying. It's a crying like it is all inside my face, seeping out through my eyes and nose. If I open my mouth, I'll bawl. I just keep looking down at Joy, purring and sucking.

She didn't ask to be born. "She didn't ask to be born," I say out loud. Then I cry through my mouth, open and selfish. Joy's eyes open just a peep, like scraps of navy cloth. Her eyelids are pink, with a tiny line of blond eyelashes. Looks like Alamand has tried to draw her some hair and come up with a heart-shape of fuzz too low on her forehead.

"What's gone happen to Mama?" I say, saying it to myself, breathing in and shuddering. Earl don't say nothing, kind of rocks to his toes; his boots squeak and he sets them flat on the floor. The kitchen spigot makes a cracking sound, bout to thaw or bust, one.

"How long can he keep her like that?" I ask, meaning the undertaker, Mama in cold storage.

When Earl don't say nothing this time, I look up at him and see his spoked blue eyes watering up, tears running down his jaw and dropping on his light yellow shirt.

"I better cut the damper on that fire, don't you think?" He goes over to the pipe and twists the lever on the damper.

The fire has been roaring in my ears and I didn't know it. Now it muffles and sings. The potbellied sides get red, like somebody's cheeks blushing. I can see the fire, like mingling red and yellow color crayons, through a crack in the side.

"I do wish she could be buried on Sunday," I say, "just like anybody else that died middle of the week." I rest my head on the top of the rocker and gaze at the ceiling. Where the rain has leaked, it has bulked up the tongue-and-groove boards. Moldy patches what keep the house smelling musty. "I ain't never minded being poor till now. Even at school, I didn't mind having to sign up for free lunches. Not having nothing fitting to wear. I just studied all that much harder to make good grades so I could go off to be a teacher and show everybody. I ain't never even made a B, you know that? Being ugly don't even bother me."

He clears his throat, but I don't look at him. I know he thinks I'm cute: freckles, snaggled teeth, and all. Below my right eye, two freckles, chained together, look like a teardrop. "My teeth hurts and I don't even care," I say to spite him for being stupid, to spite him for killing them robins—to spite the old man, the whole world. "Next week I belong to see the county tooth dentist at the health department, behind the old man's back. And I know I can't go now. Before, I could just picture myself with good teeth like Mandy Moore's."

I don't care where Earl is listening or not. I just want to say it. I feel good, like the crying and jabbering is getting rid of a poison in my system. I know he don't have no remedy, no more than I do, no more than the tooth dentist does. But I know Earl will listen. I keep rocking, saying whatever comes to mind. "When I was little and lost a tooth and put it under my pillow," I say, "Mama would tell me the tooth fairy come but couldn't find it, and that's how come he didn't leave me no money."

In a minute, I hear Earl's boots scraping across the floor, and I look back. He is carrying the three soggy-feathered robins by the feet. He goes out the front door like he come in, like somebody slipping around.

Old Man

When I come out this morning, weren't a soul stirring but a bunch of trifling squirrels, fussing in the gums on Troublesome Creek. But to be on the safe side, I eased the door shet and hobbled off the cement slope like I couldn't hardly get up and go (I am ailing; bum knee's acting up). I give hit another minute for a car slowing at the red light; hit picked up speed, passing me, and headed down the dip in the hardroad where the county's drove a line of white stobs on the shoulders to keep people from running off in the creek. I yawned and stretched, then moseyed on down to the creek to do my business, then headed for the dumpster across the hardroad where the sun coming up shines in the pines.

First thing in the morning, generally, they's a long string of transfer trucks from the café to the house, pulled over for the night with their motors idling (keeps from wasting gas, they say). Then they'll head out Upnorth, smoke fumes and racket lingering till good day. Most mornings, I'd be done out trying to learn what-all they been up to, where they come from and where they're off to; fureigners don't talk all that much. But this morning I give 'em time to clear on out while I took my second cup of Luzianne coffee. When the last one pulled out, I figgered I better slip on over to the dumpster before the county come and hauled off the garbage; and then, to look good, I'll slip on back in the house before that aggravating bunch of women comes toting in more vittles.

Hain't like hit used to be. At the old county dump in the woods close to Tarver, a man could take his time and pick over stuff without worrying about the county hauling hit off before he got around to hit. Well, as Buck says, that's progress. From Cornerville to Swanoochee Creek, I work some twenty-odd dumpsters a week, busting a gut reaching over the sides, handling other people's nastiness, and looking out for them old propped-up lids. Hit hain't easy.

Wish I could come up on a old pocketbook with two hundred smackers in hit. Nope, I hain't getting into hit! That's the boys' place to bury their mama. If they waiting on me, they backing up. I hain't got no money and don't want none; if the good Lord had meant me to be a rich man, he'd of had Uncle John leave his money to me and not the county. Buster's got hit now. And I hain't paying no taxes. I hain't got no use for no land but the six-foot strip I'll come by natural when I die. I done went all out on Becky; let the boys look out for their mama. As hit is, I'm gone leave this old world owing on one funeral; I don't aim to leave here owing on two. Can't get blood out of a turnip.

I sneak on out in the bushes, coming up on the backside of the dumpster, so nobody hanging around the court-house won't spot me. Hit's a known fact I plunder in dumpsters. I just don't want that bunch over there seeing me out and moving while Louella's laying a corpse in Jasper. Hit might give them the idear I'm able to take on another funeral bill. I hain't. If ery one of 'em wants to chip in, they're welcome to. So far, they hain't done noth-ing but tote in vittles for Loujean to have to put up. I hain't a bit above taking a handout, just not from the county, meaning Buster. By rights, that money's as much mine as hit is his'n: Uncle John fixed hit that away for all the Scurvys. He knowed if he'd just left hit to us straight out, we'd of throwed hit all away. Like hit is, we oughta be able to draw on his money along and along—being county people like we are and always was and will be. But Buster goes and beats us out of what's coming to us. Well, I hain't worrying myself into a early grave.

I reach over in the dumpster and pull out a black silk wrop. A necklace made of real sea shells falls out when I shake hit. I make a lunge for the necklace and have to let hit go, so I can duck down when I see Alamand come loaf-ing along the courtyard. I don't want to run up with him. Buddy-buddy, him and that Earl. Bringing him home to eat up my vittles. I bout cleaned house a while back. What they think this is, a hotel? Soon as Louella gets put away, I'm gone have to run Earl off again.

I wait for Alamand to straggle across the road, heading for Hoot's store, and then I reach back in the dumpster around a milk carton and some egg hulls, trying to lay hold of that necklace. The shells rattle and slide on down around the neck of a cocoaler bottle on the bottom. I can't reach hit. I jack my bum knee up on the side of the dump-ster and hiest myself up, leaning over in hit with my face in a pile of coffee grinds and ketchup. Bout the time I get my hands on the necklace and start to back out, my knee jerks and knocks the lid of the dumpster, *kawop!* on my back. A hot white light goes off in my head; everything goes black. If I had any teeth, I'd of bit my tongue clean off. My face is mashed down in that pile of coffee grinds and ketchup.

I wiggle around, my good leg going numb where hit's caught betwixt the lid and the lip of the dumpster, giving me a little crack of light. I can't move. Lord God amighty! I work my way down like a gopher in a hole and go to groaning, but the groans don't go nowhere. My right ear is sawing up against something sharp—maybe a axe, or a hoe blade. I hope hit don't cut off my ear, and I hope hit's a axe since the one at the house is been busted out of the han-dle. (Earl was chopping wood for Louella and didn't know how; that's how come hit to be busted out of the handle.)

I get still, figgering to save my breath. If I holler nobody likely won't hear me and I'll be using up what lit-tle dab of air is left in here. Besides, I don't want to chance nobody catching me like this, not with Louella laying a corpse and me belonged to be in mourning. What if Sonia Lee was to come walking up? I don't want her to catch me with coffee grinds and ketchup on my face, my ear half cut off, my good leg sticking out like Howdy Doody hanging from his trunk. What if the county comes by to dump the dumpster? I'll be in a heck of a fix. I go to working myself around on my back—hit's a axe all right. I feel hit sticking in my back now. My good leg's still hanging out, numb or cut off one. But I get to where I can push up on the lid with both hands and shove with all my might. The trash bogs down, me with hit, the axe gouges in my back.

Except for that one crack of light, hit's dark. But even if hit weren't, I couldn't see for coffee grinds in my eyes. My nose too. I blow hard and the grinds fly out of my nose, into my mouth—ketchup coffee. Maybe I can't get no air cause they hain't none in here. What if I'm dying? I go hot all over. I hain't never really thought about dying before. I make light of hit generally, but I hain't really give hit much thought. I always figgered I'd go right after Louella, or about the same time, but the both of us would be old and wore out by then. I hain't.

That sets me on fire. I hain't going like this, not this easy. I get to twisting and rocking, trying to kick the side of the dumpster with my good foot hanging out. Let somebody know I'm in here.

I stop. Wait a minute! Maybe somebody'll come along—not Buster—and find me. Say, one of the church ladies. Then they'll have to take pity on me and come up with the down payment on Louella's funeral. I kick harder, beating the lid with the heel of my hand at the same time. *Baloom baloom baloom* wallows down. Yeah! Miss Amaretta, or Miss Joyce, somebody from the church. They can pass the hat at church tomorrow, then the boys can run go tell the undertaker to get started. I get my one heel going—*baloom baloom baloom*—against the outside of the dumpster, and the racket drubs in my head. My face goes hot, then cold, feels wet. Maybe I'm bleeding, maybe I'm dying. I must be bleeding; that's how come the top of my head is paining. What if the county comes along and dumps the dumpster in the back of that truck, then hauls me and the garbage off to that canyon in Thistle Hammock. Nobody won't never know I was in here. They'll think I bailed out on my debt or run off to keep from taking on another one—I hain't exactly made hit no secret—that and the new baby.

I study myself. All I got to do is quieten off, not get riled, lay still and wait. You got to look on the bright side. Say, I'm laying here in this shape—bleeding, dirty, my good leg nearbout cut off—and a church lady comes by. How's she gone turn her back? She hain't. And one of them's bound to be along by and by. On Saturdays, they always running back and forth to the store for Sunday-dinner doings. Besides, they'll be toting more vittles to my house for dinner today.

I couldn't of worked hit out no better if I'd tried. I hain't got to worry about the county: the courthouse is closed on Saturdays and the garbage crew don't even work today. All I got to do is lay right here, warm and still, and wait. Yessir, sometimes hit takes something like this to turn things around. Who'd expect a busted-up, crippled old man to get out and work out another funeral, much less work for a family, a baby he hain't even ordered? Every time I paid that woman a little attention, she'd come up in the family way. I'll wait, and when the lid hoves up, I'll shet my eyes and hear Miss Amaretta let out a holler and then head for help.

Ah, now I see the crack of light growing, feel the cold air shooting in around the lid. I shet my eyes, roll out my tongue, lay my head to one side, and listen to the lid creak back.

"Uncle Lay!"

I open my eyes just in time to see that confounded Earl chunk three dead robins in on my head.

"What in the world happened to you, Uncle Lay?" He jerks back.

"Shet that lid, boy!" I say low. "And I hain't your uncle, so quit calling me Uncle Lay. Now, get on out from here."

I pick up one of the stiff robins and chunk hit back at him. He dodges. "No sir," he says, reaching in for my arm. "I can't just leave you like this. Come on."

"Get out from here, boy!" I say louder and jerk my arm from his hand. "You hain't got no business around here."

"You're bleeding, Uncle Lay," he says. "Come on up from there."

I kick at him with my bum leg, just miss him.

"You just grieving bad, Uncle Lay," he says. "It'll be all right. Come on, give me your hand."

I come to my feet then, pick up the axe, and chunk hit at him, just missing him by a hair. He ducks, stands up. "You got a broke heart's what it is, Uncle Lay," he says, misery writ all over his fool face.

"I'm gone break your heart, boy!" I holler, slipping in something mushy on the bottom of the dumpster, and then I scamper out. "Hain't no peace to be had around here."

"I'm gone run tell Cousin Buster yonder you're bad hurt."

I look over in front of the courthouse, and there sets that S.B. in his blue pickup with the cover on the back, watching the whole thing.

I run Earl down before he gets to the red light, me and him tussling in the grass.

Alamand

Earl's the one give me the day off from work, despite Buck's griping. Guess my old buddy figgered I'd be grieving (besides, Pee Wee jumped on me last night and I'm all stove up). I am grieving, but since it don't show, I don't guess I'm grieving like I belong to be. If I go too deep, I'm scared of what might come out. I might start shaking and can't stop. I'm shaking some now, but I know I won't be when I get to Aunt Becky's and set down to draw.

What will I draw today?

It'll come.

I walk faster, coming up on the courthouse square where the new phone booth stands by the walkway to the new flat-top courthouse. The post office, across 94, is new and flat too, both of them red brick. But arrowing up to the cold blue sky, other side of the post office from the house, the steeple on the old Methodist Church sets off something I can't name but just feel—all that old and new!—like heat under glass. I hurry now, crossing 129 to get a better picture of the new courthouse in front of the old hotel. I can't wait to find out what the picture will be, like putting a jigsaw puzzle together without looking at the box top.

Coming out the door of Hoot's old cement-block store and heading for the new courthouse, Miss Amaretta, my pick of the lunchroom ladies, bumps into me. "Bless your lil ole heart!" she says and hugs me.

"How you, Miss Amaretta?" I hug her back, smelling the old on her—talcum? She's bad about hugging me, even in the lunch line at school, and I always hug her back, right in front of everybody. She makes the best soup, always saves me seconds.

"I'm just on my way home to put on dinner to take to your house," she says, holding me by the shoulders now. "Just come to the store after a fryer."

"Prechate it, ma'am."

"I'm so sorry to hear about your mama," she says, her watered-gray eyes searching my lying face. She pulls me back to her soft drooped bosom. Her hair is white and poufy as a wind cloud; she's taller than Buck, more man-like than woman, except for being mooshy. I can feel the cold wrapped chicken on my back.

"Sugar," she says, "I been missing you in the lunch line here lately. How come?"

"Teacher's been making me stay in the room for cutting up," I say. She knows I'm storying.

"Listen here," she says, "don't you let worrying over your mama interfere with your schooling, you hear? Louella wouldn't of wanted that. I'm gone do all I can to help out."

"Yes ma'am. We shore prechate it."

I feel like Pinocchio: I been laying out of school for the past six weeks. She kisses me on the cheek—she smells like nothing really—not a old kiss or a young kiss. I let her have at it, all the time gazing off at the old brick, two-story Masonic Lodge north of Hoot's store. I look across 129 again at the new flat brick courthouse and think about the old biscuit-white two-story courthouse they just tore down. Oaks and all. They did leave one. I get confused and lose the picture in my head.

Miss Amaretta's still smooching on me.

I don't know how it ended up, how I got a-loose from her, since now I'm heading along the school-bus shortcut, passing the new brick jailhouse, south side of the court-yard, trying to recollect the old yellow Gulf filling sta-tion—did it have a upstairs room?—used to set on the cor-ner facing the jail, where now they've put up a new flat brick health department in its place.

Why did they put up so many two-story buildings back then? And why are they tearing them down? Does every-body hate old, love new? What does all this old and new stuff mean? Who are they? The county? If that's the way of it, I'm a they too and not a I like I'd thought.

I get the picture again, so I take off trucking past the hotel, then past three or four more look-alike houses, and then Buster's house, praying Aunt Ida Mae don't pop out her back door and stop me. I keep my eyes on the old red brick schoolhouse, dead on Saturdays, unless somebody's throwing a shindig. Red brick? Shouldn't it be block or board if it's old? And it is old, I know for a fact. What's with the bricks? I feel confused again and start to turn around and go to Aunt Ida Mae's to watch cartoons on her TV.

I go on.

Where the new blacktop road quits in front of the schoolhouse, a old dirt road picks up. My head hurts. I turn the corner, at the old smoking tree, its shadow flared on the packed dirt and patchy grass, and follow the straightaway into the quarters, set facing the school grounds, where I go when I want to.

Why did they put the quarters there behind the old white school? Which is oldest, which is newest? I need to know. But I have faith that I'll know it all, make it whole, soon as I get to Aunt Becky's and put it all down on paper. Just like I have faith Mama'll get buried, one way or another. I have faith that when I draw my picture, I'll know how come she died and how come I can still roam around on Saturday morning with her dead and the birds still tweeting same as they done last Saturday and will the next Saturday. It's like being God, making a world where things fit.

Old Lucious, setting on the porch of one of the side-by-side shanties, to my right, starts his stuff with me: treating me like I'm obliged to stop and run off at the mouth with him. If I don't he'll think it's cause he's colored. And it's not. I like him. I just wish he liked me stead of playing up to me like coloreds do whites. "Where you be off to in a big hurry?" he calls, gumming and rocking with his spider legs crossed.

"Checking on Aunt Becky's place for her," I say, kicking around in his sandy yard. Bits of glass glitter in the sun; the wind's died down since yesterday, but it's colder.

"You a right smart boy, yo'self," he says, brushing his hands on the arms of the rocker.

I know he don't mean it, but I act like I think he does and try to make sense out of how coloreds and whites go on at one another over nothing. I've never heared a white man and a colored man talk sense together. A white man gives a order and a colored man can't wait to carry it out. I know it's a lie.

Once I found a colored newspaper full of hate talk about whites. Scared me to death! And for a while I'd cut through the woods to Aunt Becky's, but then I figgered they was all too scared to hurt anybody. If they wadn't, how come they didn't talk back and read their newspapers out in the open.

"I best be going," I say and jump over old Lucious's washpot, since that's what he expects me to do—I've always done it.

"Be coming back," he says, and I think how I ain't never really been in the first place.

I'm itching now, the back of my neck's burning. I've got too much and not enough to draw from. The picture might not come when I get there. What if I can't get it out?

A bunch of colored younguns is running across the shanty yards, hollering. I hope they don't mess with me this time. I don't generally mind; I talk to them. And being younguns, they don't know to play up to me like old Lucious. We just talk, not about nothing, but just anything comes up. Like how come I ain't in school, how old I am. Me and one of 'ems got the same birthday. Stuff like that.

The best I ever drawed was a picture of them playing on a truck inner tube; got it from the middle, like I was God up above looking down on a patch of sunflowers opening up. I had to throw the picture away, of course, so nobody wouldn't see it and laugh at me. I couldn't never of made nobody see what I meant by it. I wish I'd of had a secret place to put it away; I do wish that. I can still see it in my mind, but I couldn't never go back and draw it again. When I'm done, I'm done, and the picture in my mind's wore out.

About halfway along the semicircle of shanties, I take a right fork in the road, tracked with bare feet, and pass the tiny Church of Sinners where Mama used to go. I can smell mold on the cement-block walls and the green of cedars growing each side. I know the funeral will be here. I know she'll have one. I don't feel one bit guilty for not setting around and worrying my head off with the rest of the family. If they'd stop and think about it, they'd know one way or the other she'll get buried. Just like Aunt Becky about five years ago, at half what her funeral cost. That was the old man's doings. And for once he done a fine thing, in my estimation. He could of buried her for a lot less. I'm beholding.

If I let myself get hung up on thinking about Aunt Becky dying, I'll be drawing the wrong thing. Or does that fit in here too, with the other stuff storming in my head? I have to keep that separated, else I'll be mixing up facts with my fantasies. I hate facts. That's how come I'm failing school, much as anything. But if they give grades for drawing fantasies in school, I'd pro'bly fail anyhow, since most of my fantasies don't make sense either. Just like Pee Wee with his likker, I'm hooked on drawing.

Earl

_____ When looked like, Friday night, wadn't nobody gone scare up enough money to put Loujean's mama away, and the whole bunch fighting amongst theirselfs, I decided wadn't nothing left to do but get in touch with Aunt Louella's sister Annie Bell, who my mama'd told me lived in Etlanna. I figgered anybody lived in Etlanna had to be rich.

Coming home from The Line, Pee Wee'd done jumped on Alamand, me playing referee and driving the post truck, then Buck jumped on all of us for being gone so long, and now Uncle Lay . . . I don't know if Loujean'll ever get over them robins. A dumb thing to do and I own up to it. But didn't seem all that dumb at the time.

Just like calling up that Annie Bell lady didn't seem dumb at the time, but'll pro'bly turn out to be dumb before Saturday runs into Sunday. Mark my words, as my old man used to say, when he'd light in on me about getting a education after I quit school last year.

Still I can't name off nobody in Swanoochee County's got a diploma for dipping gum and hauling fence posts and pulpwood. No farmers or loggers neither, though they make a go of it. Looks to me like grownups around here is always preaching education, but if us boys was to stay in school wouldn't none of our folks be able to do without our dollar or so kicked in at the end of the week.

Anyhow, tore up as he was on Friday night, bless his heart, pore lil ole Alamand went snooping through his dead mama's cigar box of old letters and come up with a last name and address for his Aunt Annie Bell, who he ain't never laid eyes on but once. I told him the address was for my mama, wanting to write to this Aunt Annie Bell. He just scratched his head and wandered back in the house, leaving me standing in the alley between the post office and Buster's old store.

It long about midnight then, I headed out for the courtyard, strolling around the square a time or two, trying to get up the nerve to mingle with them old rough boys that hang around Hoot's store facing the courthouse across 129. Just setting there every weekend on the cement parking space in their pickups, guzzling beer and listening to the Big Ape radio station out of Jacksonville, Florida. Real loud. News about President Kennedy, who looks like a sissy on the TV but ain't. They say. Then more rock and roll, and about every other song, that old ape goes to bellering: *Ah-ee-ah!* Fellow by the name of Roman Candle was one of them, who I'd done had a run-in with at school before we quit. About him making eyes at my girlfriend Libby, best I recall. I've been in and out of love all my life, it's a fact, but I think Loujean's gone wrap up my wild days.

Hands in my jacket pockets, to keep my fingers from freezing off, I took another turn around the courthouse square, gazing up at the stars pricking the cold sky and listening to that ape beller, and for some reason remembering the winter I turned fifteen and took a furlough from school to bed land ahead of the sapling-setting crew for Cato Timber Company. Driving that great big vibrating crawler tractor and bedding harrow over fresh-cleared ground where the Alapaha River was running right up under me. Just north a piece from where I was working, out of Jennings, Florida, the river flows under a wall of soaprock and then nothing but planted pines for a mile or two, then all of a sudden that tea-colored water comes gushing out of a soaprock shelf, flows on for maybe another rivermile where the Alapaha River stops forever and the Suwannee River starts.

Throughout the day, I'd happen up on a pool of black boiling water in the rooty, raw dirt to remind me the river was still running under me and my tractor. I was looking anytime for the ground to give way and the river to swallow me up.

Old Man lived not far from there would keep reminding me too. He'd step out of the woods like a haint and holler, "Son, you gone get killed out there!"

"Naw," I'd mouth back and laugh and keep driving, so scared my jaws was locked.

I stopped walking in front of the courthouse, facing them lined-up pickups across 129. If I hadn't been killed bedding land on top of that river, I didn't reckon I'd be killed by a bunch of jokers jumping on me, and me with no pocketknife.

Ah-ee-ah!

I took off walking, straight across the hardroad, straight up to the middle truck, where I could see Roman Candle's keen, pimply face through the windshield flashing red from the blinking red light at the crossing. Fishing out my Old Timer that Daddy give me a long time ago, the same knife his daddy give him a long time ago. I clutched it in my right hand, fingering each blade with its own stories and lies. "What's doing, Roman Candle?" I said.

"Just messing around," he said and rolled his eyes at the blond boy bracing a can of Bud on the steering wheel.

"I got a little business to talk over with you," I said, holding out the knife, then figgered he might think I'd come to gut him, so added quick, "Need a little pocket change and looking to sell my Old Timer. You innerstid?"

"Not specially," he said and spit on the cement at my feet.

But wadn't long before he give me a dollar and took the knife. I had to go through three or four more of them old rough-looking boys before I got me enough change to make the call to that Annie Bell lady from the new telephone booth in front of the courthouse. Them all watching me, knowing I was from now on and forever as defenseless as a widder woman.

I'm afraid the call wadn't worth it.

This Annie Bell lady come on the telephone after two or three rings and went to going "Who? Who?" every time I tried to tell her my name. I figgered I'd done enough sinning already to send my soul to hell, so I told her I was the Swanoochee County sheriff calling with some bad news. She went to saying "What? What?" and me all primed to break it to her easy that her sister had died, so I just come on out with it and she asked me who killed her sister: "Who? Who?"

"Nobody," I said.

"What? What?" she said again, and I told her again that her sister had died and she bout bit my head off: "You stupid, redneck idiot, I'm asking what did she die of. Don't tell me she had another baby!" I didn't.

What she said next—or mumbled as I was hanging up the telephone—was how come me to believe selling my Old Timer wadn't worth it: "Lord, let me call up Rosanne and see if I can get me a way to go."

Alamand

— — — — — — — — — — Coming round the curve
at Rayford Sharp's, I can see the clearing behind his junk
cars where Aunt Becky's place sets off to itself, the last
house and then woods. The unpainted two-room cabin
that ain't nobody lived in since she died is centered on the
open yard, wind-swept dirt like concrete with a couple of
bony-looking crepe myrtles. The wind's shishing way off in
the pines now. I listen and let it suck me in, shutting out
the racket of the quarters. Stepping over the boundary
where the picket gate's been rode down, where the wire
fence slumps like crisscrossed vines, I seal off the world
behind me.

I catch hold of the porch post, warmed by the sun, and
swing up over the caved-in doorsteps. A lizard flashes like
sun on a mirror across the door. I open it a crack and stand
listening to the lonesome hollowness of the house. I can
smell dry paper. Feel like I ought not move. The unpainted
walls are silvery gray from the light spilling through the
smeary window on the east side of the room. Dust fraz
shapes the air into something you can see, spiriting up

from the graveyard of notebook paper and cardboard drawings on the floor.

Somebody's been pilfering through Aunt Becky's midget dresser and chest, keeping clothes they wanted and casting the rest on the floor. A dull aluminum pan with a mending patch on the bottom puddles light on a layer of drab aprons and frocks. Most of the papers is stuff I drawed and give to her before she died; the rest is what I done after she died—like B.C. and A.D. they teach you in school. I know which pictures from which, and yet I can't hardly keep up with the months of the year.

I set down on the floor, listening to the cabin creaking. Outside, a woody dead althea bush brushes the windowpane, like it's trying to fool me into believing it'll bloom again. I start checking papers for a clean sheet, sailing them off in the dust fraz: a picture of a fat Mr. McGoo I drawed when I used to copy the funny papers; a armless woman in a dress down to her ankles, when I went through trying to draw Aunt Becky; a picture of a beer bottle, when I couldn't come up with a picture in my head. I scramble all the papers, and everlast rat-nibbled sheet's got something on the front and back, even as to a scalped corner of ribbed cardboard.

I stand up and kick around till I come up on a yellow pencil with the eraser gnawed off. I done that. I pick it up. The point's broke off, showing a hull of shaved wood. The pencil's short. I take out my pocketknife and sharpen the point, hearing the whisper of shavings on paper, while keeping my eyes on a block of sun forming near the left corner of the west wall. When I get the pencil sharp to suit me, and the block of sun beams in a perfect square on the unpainted wall, I tip over and rest my right fist on a board with the pencil at eye level. My hands are too shaky, the square's too scrunched, my pencil's too short to make the big picture building in my head. I start anyhow, with faith that my hands will get study, with faith that the frame of sun will scroll to the right as the sun moves, with faith that the pencil will last. Soon as I put the point to the smooth silvery board, my hands get study. I'm drawing. I start anywhere, with faith. Making careful feathery strokes, I work up a low square building, shading in the shingle roof, plate-glass windows on each side of the front door with streaks on the glass to show grease film. Then I make a sign on it with a fat cartoon character—one I made up—chomping down on a hamburger fatter than he is.

Soon as I get the café shaded in just right with a big overhanging oak, I move on up 129, left to right, filling in with a couple of houses on the straightaway to Hoot's store. The gravel roads come out just fine, signs and shadows (I fade out on the shortcut to 94, running west behind the store, since I don't aim to draw to the river bridge).

My pencil's holding out, working, making; I'm moving, the sun's moving, giving me more room. I hope I don't run into them shadows near the right corner.

Left to right of 129, I make Hoot's store, cement block; the courthouse, across from it; the Masonic building beside it; the red light at the crossing; the shutdown store where we live behind it, wide windows, dusty, the sign bleached wordless and dangling on one hook; the post office—new brick and flat—next to the old store; the grassed alley between the post office and our place; the tall bays and sweetgums popping up from Troublesome Creek, which I don't have to make since the water don't show from where I'm at in my head.

Circling back to the courthouse, hand eager and set, I fill in the sidewalk in front of the courthouse with the new telephone booth, even the black telephone. The railing of white metal pipes bordering the courtyard. I use up half my pencil lead making Earl leaning against the phone booth. He looks right, smiling with one leg crossed over the other.

I go on, hand brushing the wall to slide the sunlight farther over. It won't move; I'm running into dark, sharp off the sunny rectangle, and I'm running into a corner too. I can't chance thinking about running out of sun space; I'm turning a corner anyhow at the crossing, that picture in my head, so it works out fine.

I feel all right.

With study hands now, I draw the Methodist Church with its cone steeple, the cord of the old bell shadowed on the door off the stoop. Doing fine. I make up the rest of the houses to the schoolhouse: most of them easy, lofty, look-alike houses, white frame with green roofs. I wish I had a green pencil to make the roofs and the green grass, the way they balance, green to green.

The sidewalks look fine with plain pencil, specks in the concrete. A few trees here and there, all of the yards shady. (I don't mess with the block of houses where Buster lives, that or the bus route; I wonder if I should. No, I can't do that shortcut and this route to the old schoolhouse too. And I want to do the old schoolhouse from the front, working back behind it to the quarters.) I can't keep on drawing east along Highway 94, past the schoolhouse to Tarver—or I'll lose my focus. So I just sort of fade out the road and deep woods running on to Tarver. It's pretty dull going out that way anyhow. Earl's mama lives out there, but that don't have nothing to do with this; ain't no wall wide enough anyhow to draw all the pinewoods in Swanoochee County.

The cemetery and other houses, running west from the red light on 94 to the river, are another problem, but I tell myself they don't fit here either. Or do they? I feel like I've left something necessary out, a lot, but especially the old hotel. It's real old, the oldest building in Cornerville.

I turn the corner in my head, wish I'd already reached the other corner of the room, to make the picture look more real. What if I don't make it real, like the picture in my head? Nobody cares. Nobody'll see this anyhow. What if it don't fit? It don't matter; I'm just drawing for myself. But I know I'm good.

Pee Wee

_____ **N**ext thing I know, I'm waking up beside Sonia Lee with a bedsheet bunched under my chin. I lay still and watch the sunshine wiggling on the ceiling. Looks like it's glancing off water. I'm rocking, and I feel like I'm back on ship out of Inchon Landing, gazing up from my bunk at the bulkhead, waiting on high tide. I like the feeling, though I know it's just the sun glancing off the windshield of Sonia Lee's junked Mercury in the yard. But I didn't like the feeling when I was at Inchon Landing. Like everything else, a good feeling don't have no basis behind it.

I look over at Sonia Lee. Stringy blond hair spilling from her pillow onto the gray-striped bed ticking. I reach out and touch her hair, rub a strand between my fingers. A better feeling than staring at the sun on the ceiling and letting yesterday, anyday, take the place of now.

I try to figger what day this is, what time it is—I know it's morning—what's bugging the hell out of me. And then I know: it's Saturday, Mama's dead (old man finally did her in), the undertaker won't bury her without a couple hundred up front.

Anybody want to buy a gold-plated Purple Heart? Sonia Lee let me in on a little secret. I think it's a lie. The only truth is yesterday, gone; tomorrow is nothing. I wonder if I killed her.

I was everybody's favorite till I come home shot-up and full of dope. In Korea, I was a number on a dog tag.

Hair don't have no feeling in it. I keep rubbing it. Her back is to me. I can't see her breathing. I raise up and watch her long, pale arm, her hand on the ratty quilt covering her, coated-wax bones. I don't want to wake her up if she's just sleeping since that's the only time she's innocent-looking. A innocent whore? I laugh low. I need to know if she's dead or not. I know I can't depend on my recollection all that much, but if I can recollect the other stuff, important stuff, I should be able to recollect if I killed her. My head hurts too bad to think, so I let it go and think about thinking, how it works: important bad stuff jumping up at you when you open your eyes. The only time it don't is when you're passed-out drunk.

I lay back on my pillow, keeping the hair. Hangs halfway down her back where her waist slopes off to her round butt. Like me, she's about starved herself to death. Smoking dope, laying drunk; I wish I had a nickel for every meal we've made out of whiskey and dope.

Her being a whore don't make me think no less of her; we're all whores.

Earl can stick up his nose if he wants to. I beat Alamand's ass for him last night—I can recollect that—and should of beat Earl's too. I call her Wildcat. She didn't come from around here. Home girls is worse, a bunch of teases, looking to get married. Wildcat ain't got no plans.

She knows the truth about tomorrow, the lie. Laying there, not trying to recollect nothing, since it don't matter really—not even if she's dead—her secret comes to me: the old man is a regular customer of hers. My eyeballs get hot; I feel like I need to puke. I ease out.

She's playing possum.

Loujean

———————— I put the baby down after her bath and get myself a mouthful of Miss Amaretta's chicken and rice. Quiet, at last.

Long about dinnertime, she dropped off a whole box of food, fussed over the baby, then took off home in a hurry, saying she'd be right back. Two or three ladies from the Methodist Church come in after that with a pound cake and some casseroles. Aunt Ida Mae sent Thelma with a bowl of collard greens, some brisket stew, and a loaf of hoghead cheese.

Thelma set and rocked the baby while I run over to the courthouse and drawed a bucket of water. When I come back, she was painting her fingernails with her hands spread on the baby in her lap, it just a-bawling.

Me and Thelma's cousins, both in the same grade at school. She's the only real girlfriend I've got. But Earl's my best friend now, since I poured my heart out to him this morning; he's the one who knows the real me. Still and all, me and Thelma goes way back, used to play every day together. I wish we could go back to them days when we would play house in the broomsage patch. We'd clear out a spot with Aunt Ida Mae's hoe and rake and make different rooms. Had a kitchen and all with Thelma's play stove and Frigidaire set. We couldn't wait to grow up and get married.

Sometimes we'd get tired of staying in—the sky for a ceiling, the broomsage for walls—and we'd go out and gather coffeeweeds, stripping off the layers of limp green leaves. We'd stack them like dollars, counting them like they do at a bank. We was rich.

Summer days, we'd set on the hot sidewalk in front of the old store and play jackstones. The flats of our bare feet pressed together to hem up the ball and jacks, gnats scabbing over the festering sores of impetigo on our linked legs. Seems like the worst thing we had to worry about back then was mad dogs—our mamas would always warn us to look out for mad dogs when we left the house.

Thelma's gone boy crazy now. Popping gum, running her radio wide open, gashing her heel strings with her daddy's razor. Ain't nothing she loves better than dancing to the jukebox at the café. I know Miss Annette's sick and tired of her, and Aunt Ida Mae's bout to pull her hair out. But I like watching Thelma like that, or did till I caught her painting her fingernails on the baby. It's like she's doing stuff I wouldn't dare do and couldn't do nohow. Not just cause I don't have no transistor radio or nail polish. Oh, I could use hers, sure, but I wouldn't know how to go about acting free like that. When you got all these troubles at home, your mind ain't free to hang loose and cut up. She's got her troubles too, but the difference is they don't bother her. She's the one person I don't have to feel ashamed of the old man and Pee Wee around. She knows them, they're her own kin (she's big on kinfolks), she's used to it. "What you gone do with the baby?" she asked me when I got back from the courthouse.

I slid the baby from underneath Thelma's Fire Engine Red nails. "I'm gone take care of her," I said, toting the baby to the bed. I practically had to roll her out of the blanket to get her a-loose; that's how tight the blanket was tucked, the way Miss Maggie, the county nurse, had showed me to wrap her.

"By yourself?" asked Thelma.

"Right by myself." I'd made up my mind and I wadn't backing off for nobody. I'd cried my last. The baby sucked in and got quiet, no sound but the fire in the stove crackling. I thought she was fixing to lose her breath, but she didn't.

"How you going to school and do that?" Thelma's frosty-pink lips parted. I could see her thin bluish teeth. Her lips is too skimpy so she fills them out with lipstick. Her fine blond hair is bushed like cotton candy.

"I'm not going back to school," I said.

She propped both feet on the bottom rung of the rocker, blunt knees high. "Maybe you oughta get married."

I could tell by the look in her close-set green eyes she was sorry for me and didn't want me to know it, didn't know how to say how sorry.

"What would I want to get married for?" I said.

"If you don't, they're liable not to let you keep it," she said. "You upset about your mama?" I made like I didn't hear her and went on stripping the baby's tiny gown with a drawstring on the tail. She was full and limp, trying to sleep at last. I had to hurry. Her stomach was pooched and blue-veined, like ink scribbles. Had I overfed her? I'd been worried I might not feed her enough.

Miss Maggie had come by yesterday evening and told me what to feed the baby. I got it down in writing, "the formula," as she called it. She come up with all kinds of stuff to test me on. I made out like I done knowed it, to make me look good, while she swabbed around the raw stump of the baby's nabel, and then her ears (she didn't never stop squalling the whole time, face blood-red, like a balloon bout to bust). Miss Maggie didn't pay her ery bit of mind; she just snatched her up like a sack of meal and stuck her under one arm and set in scrubbing her round bald head with a stiff brush dipped in the pan of water I'd heated on the cookstove.

"Make sure the water's tepid," Miss Maggie said, "and don't scrub too lightly."

She was talking above the baby's racket while I back-tracked over her lesson on how to wrap the baby "properly" in a "receiving blanket": spread the blanket on the bed, lay the baby in the middle of it with her head at the top corner; bring the left corner over her front and tuck it under her back, then bring the corner at her feet up and fold it under her chin. Wind the right corner clean around the baby, front to back. For going outdoors—which I couldn't picture doing—flap the top corner down over her face. A cat in a croker sack would stand a better chance of getting a-loose. I looked at the baby clamped under Miss Maggie's arm, kicking against that white starched uniform while Miss Maggie scrubbed her head. It had to hurt.

"Moderation," Miss Maggie said, scooping water on

the baby's head; her blond fuzz looked like wet feathers on a biddy.

Miss Maggie always used that word "moderation"; I wouldn't never use it, but I wouldn't never forget it neither. Last year at school, somebody come up with the idear for her to learn us girls a sex-education class. (Most of us had just started—our periods—and what they really meant to do was learn us how to take care of ourselfs, I think.)

Miss Maggie had marched us off to the dark room—I guess so the boys couldn't peep in the windows—where we generally went to watch shows on how to take care of our teeth. It took her a whole hour to talk around talking about sex. She kept using proper words like "moderation," which didn't get down to nothing. She did use the word "vagina" once, and "penis"! All the girls was sniggering with their heads down.

Miss Maggie didn't pay them ery bit of mind, just kept standing up there in front of the white picture screen, waving a pointer like she was learning us geography. She was giving a talk on what she called our "personal grooming."

"And don't forget to oil it," she said to me now.

"Ma'am?" I said, watching her pour oil on the baby's raw scalp, then rub it around in a circle.

"Cradle cap," she said. Her sharp face was as clean and stiff as her uniform. I'd do it all, just like she said, if it killed me. But I had a feeling Miss Maggie got all she knowed from some book. I knowed she hadn't had no babies of her own. And she, of all people, sure wouldn't of had sex.

*   *   *

I oiled the baby's head—her second bath in two days, which felt like forty—doing my best to keep the oil out of her eyes, while Thelma set watching. I was glad she was there since it made things seem normal. Except for having a baby around; I held that against her again, but just for a second. Then I couldn't think of nothing I'd ruther be doing, no place I'd ruther be. Not even down at the café doing the shag with Thelma (she hadn't been able to get no boys to do it with her yet).

For the longest time, Thelma just set there, like she knowed I felt good with her around. Except for painting her fingernails, you'd of thought she was a old lady. Maybe, like me, she was thinking about our mamas visiting back and to, how we was acting just like them. Felt like we'd been there before, but this wadn't yesterday or tomorrow, it was today, it was now. We'd crossed a line somewhere. Thelma would cross back without me. I started to beg her to stay.

"I got to be getting home," she said, "if I can't be of no use to you."

"No, they ain't nothing," I said, covering the baby's nakedness while Thelma swung open the kitchen door. At least they ain't no wind today. But wadn't long before Mama's sisters would blow in like a storm.

Alamand

_ _ _ _ _ _ _ _ _ I hear somebody whooping and hollering way off—the colored younguns. My heart flutters. What if they come and bother me right now? I don't care if they pilfer in Aunt Becky's house, I don't blame them. I love to pilfer too, and I'm always going in empty houses and hollering to hear the bounce of my own voice, to smell the old walls, where nobody ain't been in a while.

Where was I?

I've stopped drawing.

I'm scared.

I look back over my drawing, just the last part, so I can hook on. I look back just to the corner. If I look from the beginning of the picture, I won't have no surprise when I get done, or I might get mixed up or let down. I can't wait. I have to hurry before somebody comes, or I'll lose it. I can feel the picture, like my heart beating, swelling, telling the truth.

Even with all the angles and gables of the old school-house, my pencil holds out, but I've moved on to another corner. The new wing of the school will just fit. I don't really want to turn the corner here, but that's okay. I can't let that get in the way. The whole thing's working again. I get the smoking tree down, start to put Buck up under it, smoking a cigarette, but don't. I only want Earl in the picture, alone by the telephone booth. Sweet like he is here lately. Not like he is when he follows Pee Wee and Buck off getting into stuff. You can depend on this Earl, the other Earl acts just like them. I don't put Earl there under the smoking tree either, since he ain't the kind to stand around smoking and jawing. This Earl ain't.

Soon I make my curve in the road to the quarters, draw the wire fence around the school yard. The fence posts use up too much lead and I have to sharpen the pencil again. Now the metal of the eraser scrubs the palm of my hand. The scrubbing keeps messing with me. I wish I hadn't gnawed off the eraser. I can't let that bother me though, since I'm crossing the road and filling in with the side-by-side shanties, not that they're hard to do. They all look alike. And I don't put old Lucious on the porch. I do keep the washpot I always jump over. The dirt yards and roads are fun, since they all run together and I can smell the dirt. (Had trouble with the blacktop a ways back because of the sharp oil smell in the heat and how it stopped and started for no good reason.)

I put the big oak on the curve of the road in the quarters, school-yard side of the wire fence, just like it is. Fill in the woods behind the shanties, the sky above them, with a few streaked clouds, turn the curve to the Church of Sinners—at the real corner of the room.

That is good. Each concrete block, in a shoe-box shape, I sketch out exactly; my hands couldn't be no studier, even though my pencil's running low. I want to look down for another one, but I know in my soul none won't be there. Aunt Becky didn't never write a lick, not even a letter. If I think about her stubby strong hands, I'm lost. I go on and make the roof on the church in a triangle, fill it in light— the cedars on the sides too—then the shanties back behind it, just the ones showing from the road.

I do that good, but on the one coming this a-way, I mess up for no good reason. It don't look all that different, but the space between it and the next house takes my mind off what I'm doing. The ones in the main part of the quarters are closer placed. This space between it and Rayford Sharp's makes me know a lot of space is coming up, and then Aunt Becky's off to itself, where the woods carry on to the Okefenokee Swamp and forever. Where the yard is white and open.

Across the road, in front of Rayford's, there's three or four more houses I don't want to do since I'm hurrying up now to get to Aunt Becky's. But I have to, and they don't come out like they really are; but the pines behind them look okay, merge with the sky like reflections on a lake. I give the sky a few more clouds to make up for not doing the houses justice, and feel a strong urge to stand back and look at the whole thing. I don't. I can't. My pencil's getting littler, feels like the point's stuck to the wall.

I'm shaking but my hands ain't, thank goodness!

I make Aunt Becky's yard in a round, just like she carved it out of the woods with her hoe. Perfect circle. Too perfect. Moving in, I make the circle flower beds, do the dome glass electric insulators bordering the plots, the petunias blooming like they do in the spring.

Now my hands go to shaking. I'm coming up on the well; I want to look out the window where the sun shines through and follows my picture, corner to corner and wall to wall. I don't want to see the well out the window, I want to just draw it. I need to. I start from the bottom, with the broke bricks and ragged mortar, the way the mortar's really sunk in, the sun bouncing in a soft glow off the red bricks.

I'm getting close to the top. The well's growing taller, the red well that's red only in my head. I can smell the water, ferny green, riffling and cold below.

My pencil's giving out and I'm glad. I get to the rim of the well and start specking and smearing mortar. The circle won't close; Aunt Becky's in the way, armless and squat in her long full skirts. I rub my hand on the wall to erase her. She won't move. I try to draw over her, laying the point of the pencil on the side. She jumps in the well with a wallowed-out holler, her gray skirt ballooning over my head and blocking the circle of blue sky above.

I'm down there, cold in the water.

Old Man

————————————Anybody can get the
best of Louella's sisters oughta be out whupping Japs.

I'd just set down to dinner when here comes Annie
Bell and Rosanne both, busting through the door. Didn't
get good and in the house before they lit in on me: What'd
you do to Louella? Where's our little sister at? How come
she hain't ready for viewing? When's the funeral gone be?
What's that hanging out of your nose, Lay Scurvy?

Me and the old lady wouldn't never of got along long
as we did if them two sisters of hers hadn't moved off
Upnorth.

I knowed of one place where nobody couldn't get
aholt of me—my secret fishing hole on Swanoochee
Creek. So I snuck out the back door while them two old
broads was checking out the baby. I hitched me a ride to
the flatwoods with Hamp Lee and got out at Tom's Creek
bridge, then I struck out through the woods, just a-getting
hit. I hain't never told a living soul about this place, and I
hain't fixing to. I'll die and hit my secret. When I come
out, ever so often, with a string of warmouth perch, every-

body in Swanoochee County starts picking to find out where I got 'em from. Fifty miles from nowhere, I say.

A flock of crows is scouting over the hickories in the slew, going *caw caw caw* when they spot me; a jackrabbit comes tearing out of a stand of palmettos. I can smell a buck deer; I know he can smell me. He blows at me and hit sounds like the wind in the pines. I wouldn't mess with him for nothing. He's welcome. But no man better not show his face in these flatwoods. This is mine. Stead of moping round the house, like I done yesterday, I oughta come on out here. Jabbering and carrying on, them church women didn't know I was on the place nohow. Besides, a man in mourning needs to get off to hisself. I've had a bait of people for one day.

I hadn't no more got washed up good, down at Troublesome Creek this morning, after falling in the dumpster, than here comes Pee Wee wandering up from the old Sampson Camp and busts my nose. (They's something wrong with that boy; they can blame hit on the war if they want to. I know better. I been off to war too, the first one, though hit's a known fact Uncle John did arrange me a early furlough. If anybody ever come hunting me out in these flatwoods, I don't know of hit.)

Anyhow, this morning Pee Wee just looked down off the shoulder of Troublesome Creek, spotted me, and come barreling down the ditch, jerked me up by the scruff of the neck, and socked me crazy. I just laid there, listening to the creek run, and played possum till he loped on off. Then I got up and washed again and poked the corners of my handkerchief in my nose to wick the blood and headed out to the house for a bite to eat. I was setting at the eating table, bleeding like a stuck hog, when in walks them two gussied-up broads and bawls me out. Called me a slob, a sot, good-for-nothing . . .

Well, at least I can take hit easy now, knowing them gals will put up the money for Louella's funeral. I don't know how come I didn't think about hit early on and call 'em up myself. I don't give a hang what they think about me; they too old and ugly for me anyhow. Putting on airs, like they do, I might oughta worry, though, since they pro'bly hain't got a cent to their names.

I beat me out a new path in the flatwoods, keeping a beeline southeast-and-a-little-over, to Swanoochee Creek. I step over dead limbs and take hit easy crost a bed of dead leaves so I don't leave no trail—that's the Injun in me, Creek Injun.

That's how the Swanoochee Creek come by hits name. The Injuns. I don't know how Tom's Creek got hits name. That's where I used to hang out, fishing and what-all, but after I give my fishing spot away there, I had to move on down to where the two creeks meet in a eddy black pool.

What I done was mess up and bring two old hussies from Valdosta out to my place at Tom's Creek, ten or twelve year ago. Got a little too much to drink and me and them got to riding around, cutting the fool. I'm ashamed of myself to this day for taking them out there. Weren't no better fishing nowheres. If I hadn't been drinking bad, I wouldn't never of done hit. Since that day, I don't never mix business and pleasure. I reckon I was trying to show off for them two gals. Anyhow, that morning, we cut out through the woods, south off 94, in one of them's old beat-up Plymouth; I don't know which one, didn't never even learn their names and us been together going on two days. That's how bad off I was. The gal doing the driving shut off the car and got out, going on about how she'd been hankering to go in a-bathing. Other old gal, the one in the back seat, lit out right in behind her, them both carrying on to beat all. Dove right off naked in my secret fishing hole.

I went to sobering up then. Hot as fire that day, a hundred degrees in the shade. And sick! We'd got holt of some bad shine's what hit was. I'd done got a bait of them two anyhow; they didn't look the same sober as they did and me drunk. Son! Must of been forty, forty-five, or better. Running off my fish, flouncing around in the edge under a willow where I put out my set hooks. I didn't tell 'em how many gators and snakes they was in there; I just set in the car, rared back in the front seat, burning up, sick as a dog.

"Y'all come on," I hollered, afterwhile.

They didn't pay me no mind, just swum on off crost the creek and come out buck naked on the other side, sunning around the myrcle bushes. I don't reckon no bugger'll catch a bugger, since nothing didn't mess with them. I've set a-many a time with a twelve-foot gator eyeballing me from the banks. (Wouldn't nothing like that mess with me, though, since I'm part Injun.)

"I say, y'all get on back here," I hollered. "I'm ready to go to the house."

"Aw, shut up!" one of them hollered. "He's got the blackass," the other one said, but they come dog-paddling back acrost. Washerwoman tits floating white on the black water.

"Some people don't know how to have a big time," one of them said, squirting water through her fists as she stood up.

In a minute they come wading up the bank—ugliest bunch of women I ever laid eyes on.

"Y'all come on," I hollered, "I gotta go." That was a lie and they knowed hit; anybody'd lay out two days and nights running hain't in no hurry to go nowhere.

"Crank up," one called. "We're coming."

They was peeing under a tupelo, sniggering.

I got out and went around to the other side of the car and got in, scraping sweat off my forehead and slinging hit to the dirt. The car seat was like wool, scratchy, hot, smelled like clabber and shine mixed. I switched on the car and pulled out the starter, and the engine went *chu chu chu* and quit. I tried hit again and hit done the same thing. I got out, raised the hood, tinkered around with the carburetor, then started checking the spark plugs. And just like I thought, one of 'em was bad corroded. I took out my pocketknife and started scraping hit, oil steeping on hot metal and rising to my face. Them two hussies hovering over me now.

"What happened to my car?" one said.

"What happened to my car?" I mocked.

Son! She knocked me a-winding! I didn't say nery nother word; I just done my dead-level best to keep my mind on scraping that spark plug and getting that car running. I screwed the spark plug back in the hole. They'd done got in the car, drinking in the front seat and sulling.

One of 'em said, "You want some?"

I didn't know where she was talking to me or who,

about shine or what. But I didn't. I didn't want nothing but to get shed of them two hussies. "Crank hit up," I hollered.

Old gal setting under the steering wheel give hit a try. Nothing. She cussed big. I took the spark plug out, checked hit—shiny as a silver dollar. I needed some gas to wash hit off in though.

"What you spect he was up to while we was in a-bathing?" said one of 'em; had a real gruff way of talking, both of 'em did.

"You can't never tell about his type," the other one said.

I didn't pay them no mind. I could find my way out of these woods if I took a notion to. They couldn't. Bet they didn't have nery idear where we was at. That kind of perked me up, thinking like that, but my head was busting wide open. "Y'all better look out!" I called.

"Says who?" one said. The other one was just a-grumbling.

"Either one of you gals got any string on you?" I said. A fish struck and I looked back where them gals had muddied up my fishing hole, and I seen that twelve-foot gator come nosing out of the myrcles, crossing the creek.

"What you want string for?" one said.

"To tie around this here spark plug and wash hit off with gas." They got to mumbling and flamming around inside the car. In a minute, the one with the biggest tits popped out and give me the thread out of her frocktail.

"Thank you, ma'am," I said.

"How you gone do that?" she said, backing to the bumper and leaning up. The other one—the one knocked me sidewinding—got out and stood off, watching me. Had a big gap betwixt her top front teeth.

"I'm gone show you ladies a trick," I said, winding the thread around the spark plug and tying a knot. Hit broke and I had to start over. "Now then," I said, nussing the spark plug in one hand and the thread in the other, walking around the back of the car, with them following.

I unscrewed the gas cap and dropped the spark plug down in the tank. I heard hit go *plook*, and then didn't feel no weight on the end of the thread, but I kept dabbing hit up and down like I was washing that spark plug off good.

"Ain't it washed off enough?" one said.

"Not yet," I said, thinking what I'd do next. "Hit's gotta soak a minute."

They propped up on the fender, watching me and study slapping at yellerflies. One of 'em had red wheps popping up on her moley white legs and arms.

"Here," I said, "how bout one of you ladies hanging on to this string while I step off there in the bushes and relieve myself." I passed the string to the fiery one and grabbed myself, wading out in a thick stand of gallberries.

"Feels mighty light," the old gal holding hit said, but kept on dabbing up and down with the end of the string between her thumb and finger.

"That's cause spark plugs don't weigh nothing when they're down in gas," I hollered back.

"Just keep it down there," said the other one. "I'm ready to get out of here."

"Okay."

"You want me to do it a minute?"

"I'm awright," she said, "just hot as fire. How bout knocking that fly off my arm, will you?"

Old gal doing the watching slapped the other gal hard.

"You gals keep hit down there good now," I hollered from behind a scrub oak.

"You didn't have to knock my arm off," said the one working the string.

"I didn't."

"Well, what's that blue place coming up on my arm then?" said the fiery one. "Here, you do it."

I watched till they'd switched places, then took off trucking through the woods. And they could still be there for all I know. I hain't been back to check.

Hit's warm here in this cypress slew on Swanoochee Creek; pine and cypress cuts off the wind. That other place, at Tom's Creek, weren't as fur off the road. Nobody to mess with me here. Uncle John might of left these flat-woods to the county, but I know in my heart he meant this place to be mine. You couldn't shove Buster out here. If hit weren't for the rest of the Scurvys, that S.B. could keep the money, but they got a right to what Uncle John left them for burying and all, in case of sickness. If he'd left me this big bunch of land, flat out, I'd of done chunked hit away, I own up to that. I'd of drunk hit up, or done just like I done with my Tom's Creek fishing hole, let a bunch of old hussies take over. I'm ashamed of myself. But I hain't never been one to hold no grudge against myself.

I can hear the creek running, smells fishy even off a piece. I look back at the sun—three o'clock—and get my bearings again.

"Great God! I got hit made!" I say, my voice the only voice ever been here.

I come out on a slick mud bank where the beavers and orders is been sliding, and shore nuf, there's my pole in the gallberries, just like I left hit. I find me a dead pine and peel the bark off the brown mush of sawdust. First peeling, I pick out a couple of white rubbery sawyers. Best bait— money can't buy 'em, not this kind.

I whistle now—"Dixie." Nobody hain't never whistled here but me neither. Hain't never seen sign of no man's track back in here. I bait my hook and shoot my line out, watching the white sawyer sink in the swole black water. I can see myself in hit, like a looking glass. Two dry red streaks under my busted nose, my brown baked face, my sunk eyes. Hair's sticking up like a rooster cone. Most of hit is fell out on the front. The sides is shaggy, down around my ears. "The biggest ears ever been," I say, cackling out.

I like how I sound and go to preaching: "I met the old lady back in 1920. Got hitched by the justice of the peace in his car. He come up, said get in, and I popped the question. Didn't give her the chance to say yay or nay. Over, just like that. She was crazy about me, I was crazy about her. I didn't marry no old lady."

I know the first part hain't exactly right. I'm running off at the mouth. The last part's true. I stand there, quiet all around. Me and nobody, just the water and the wind in the trees going over me.

If I didn't want nery old woman, I oughta not been messing around with her. I'm to blame. I see myself in the water, a good-for-nothing scandrel, just like her sisters said. A natural rogue. But I don't know what they want me to say about Louella, none of them. I can't tell them I loved her—but I did—when I know I'm gone get Sonia Lee to come in and wait on me right after the funeral. What they want is me crying and begging, saying I'm sorry. I am, but I hain't saying so.

I start bellering like a baby, standing up straight like I'm pissing in the water. They hain't nobody to hear, and I scrape up the tears from the pit of my soul and let them fly. Like pissing. That's what hit feels like, looks like to me, looking down. I go on like that, up straight, till the sun makes long shadows on the water from the tupelos along the bank. "I know I'm sorry," I say loud. "I know I've nearly bout starved my old lady and younguns to death. I know they hain't no forgiveness to be had." I listen to me for a while, echoing over the woods. "And when I'm done, they hain't gone be no forgiveness, Lord."

I wait, listening to the Lord in my echo. I know I mean hit, but hit sounds like a lie even to me.

"I've had a close call this morning, Lord," I say, crying, thinking I'm a lie and how much the echo sounds like a nigger preacher at big-meeting. I like hit and go on, knowing I meant hit, but knowing I'm a lie, and hit don't matter. The woods is soaking hit up, like my word-pissing is rain.

"Lord, you seen fit to take Becky and spare my least boy. You made her run jump in the well after him and lift him up to keep him from drownding, hollering every other breath, with her arms locked overhead, raised to glory. Bouncing on her toes, hollering till Earl run up on 'em and come got me and Buck."

I stand there and watch my mouth make the racket and hit's somebody else telling the truth.

"Don't I get credit, Lord, for going all out on Becky's funeral, paying extra to keep 'em from breaking her locked arms and burying her in a regular casket? Lord, you know that'd been cheaper and you know that undertaker buried her in a regular casket anyhow, being a midget like she was.

"Lord, didn't I act like a man and come up against Buster when he said he'd pay regular price but not a cent more? I didn't let 'em break them puny arms froze in place from holding up my boy. I did that one time act like a man, and I want credit, Lord.

"The other time, when I stuck a match to the corn crib with that nigger in hit, I take credit for too. But Buster and them others was the ones nailed his nutsack to the crib floor, not me. I want credit for not doing that, Lord. I didn't give that nigger no knife and tell him if he could get a-loose he was a free man. That was Buster doing the talking."

I set down on the bank and cry hit out while a jack fish swims off with my pole. Even now—the only time in my life I've been sorry—I'm just as sorry to see my pole switching off downstream with that fish that's finally got the best of me.

My nose goes to bleeding again.

My secret fishing hole hain't no more pleasure than a puddle in the yard. Where or not that nigger raped Bessie Alders, I don't know. He might of and he might not of. Hit didn't matter, not to none of us. He was uppidy. Didn't stay in his place, and back then I was a man to do Buster's bidding for the price of a liver out of a butchered hog.

"Sold my soul to the devil," I say. "I hain't had nothing to lose since. But I was honest in my heart, Lord," I beller out, coughing and staggering up the bank. "That one time, I was honest in my heart."

Buck

I come up on the old man blatting on Swanoochee Creek and ain't never been no more surprised.

It wadn't all that hard to follow him: I lost Hamp Lee's truck on a turn along the Tarver road, but I run him down and he told me to go on back to the Tom's Creek bridge and strike out southwest through that field of saplings. From there on, I just followed up the old man's whistling. Why did I come? I don't know. I reckon I just wanted to see what a half-man does while his wife's laying a corpse in cold storage. I didn't care nothing about his secret fishing hole, I was just mad. I wadn't when he come out of there, though, a broke man.

He straggles up the creek bank and spots me right off—hears me breathing or something—where I'm squatting behind a fat litard stump in the clearing. I think he's got another way of knowing stuff, besides seeing and hearing and all, what they call a sixth sense.

"What in tarnation!" he bellers and goes to backing off through the pines. "You! You S.B.!" He tumbles head over heels into a bunch of palmettos. Don't even faze him. "You follered me, trying to take over my fishing hole."

I throw up both hands, easing toward him. Me and him's got something in common now: loving Mama and hating Buster. And I'm surprised he's able to feel something, that he can cry. I never knowed that. "Old Man, hold on!" I say. "I ain't after your fishing hole."

"Bunch of rascals!" he hollers, scrambling to his feet and heading west where the sun splinters through the pines. He gazes wild-eyed around every tree for Pee Wee, Alamand, and Earl, I reckon. He's quit crying, but looks like he's been drug behind a mule. He's gray-skinned, practically blue, looks bruised, his baggy britches and shirt the same wash-water color. Cussing in letters every breath as he changes directions, west to southwest where the woods get thicker. I worry he might get lost, with it getting on toward sundown.

Crows has been study cawing ever since I come up, and I can't tell now where it's him cussing or them cawing. "Old Man!" I holler through my hands, jumping palmettos and stumps. "Wait a minute!"

He goes on, staggering like he's drunk. I stay right in behind him, close as I can, till I lose him in a thick stand of bays. I know dern well he's headed off in the wrong direction. He could run up on a bear, a rattler sunning by one of the gopher holes, or somebody's shine still. They's gators all back in these slews. "Old Man!" I holler. The crows call back, I listen. Every time I think I hear him tramping through the huckleberries, he changes directions. I think I hear him bellering in a cypress slew and cup my ear. Crows. I realize I've been circling and I've got just about enough light to get out of the flatwoods before dark. I might get lost, but he won't. He knows these woods better than me. He ain't the onliest man ever walked here, just thinks he is. Amounts to the same thing. True, don't nobody much come back in here, since it's easier to fish off the riverbanks, but they know about where he fishes at, he just don't think they know. He might be a old fool, but he's a tough one.

I take a minute to look around at the tall, stout timber, unworked, and down at the layers of rotted straw and leaves. He could be the onliest man ... I feel proud of him, and it's like coming out of a fever. He's got some shame in him, and they's honor in that.

Earl

— — — — — — — — — I turn in the phone booth so my back's to the sun and the highway, drop my last dime in the slot and dial 555-1000 for the undertaker in Jasper. ROMAN CANDLE, in pointy letters, is cut deep into the slick black paint of the phone box that now holds all my money. I wonder if he used my Old Timer.

The last aught springs the circle of numbers back slow, like gears grinding, and gives me time to clear my throat and think how to say what I have to say . . . ask.

A big transfer truck roars up to the crossing and I have to cover my free ear and holler, "Hello?" to the voice on the other end of the line.

"Yeah," I holler, "I'm calling to see what time Miss Louella Scurvy's funeral's gone be tomorrow."

Heat is building up in the glass booth, the pine tar smells strong and glues my shirt to my back.

He or she on the other end of the line hollers, "At present, no arrangements for Mrs. Scurvy's funeral have been made."

I shift a little, kissing the mouthpiece, as the transfer

revs up and roars down Troublesome Creek dip. Last straw; if this don't work, I'm gone have to go to Cousin Buster. "Well," I say, "what I'd like to do is see if I can't get a credit with you so I can make the arrangements myself."

He or she tells me to come to the funeral home and they will talk to me about the possibility.

"Wellsir," I say, hoping it's a he and not a she, "I ain't got no way to go at present."

Wrong thing to say.

He or she then asks me if I have a job.

"Yes ma'am," I say, "I cut and haul fence posts for Buck Scurvy."

Wrong thing to say.

Alamand

_ _ _ _ _ _ _ _ _ When I wake up, sundown light is shining through the open door, making a rectangle of orange on the east corner of the wall, where I ended up drawing Aunt Becky's well.

Keeping my eyes on that one spot, I set up in the rat nest of old papers and clothes and brush rice grains of rat mess from my arm. The pencil marks look like spider webs, silvery threads you have to look at close to make out. I stand up and my shadow floats like a giant's across the rectangle to the center and stops there. Where my shadow covers the sun on the wall I can make out the well. Ain't bad, but ain't done to suit me. I take my pencil—just a nub now—from behind my ear and start filling in the rim of the well, a perfect circle, with my arm braced on the wall to study my hand.

When I take a step back, my shadow covers that whole block and makes it show up good and I see I ain't made no house next to the well. So I start on the house—houses is easy to do—but when I'm done, Aunt Becky's looks just like all the other houses I've done in my head, which is behind me on the other wall, which I won't look at yet. So

I know I ain't doing it right, real looking. I lick my finger and rub the outside wall of her house, from the inside wall of her house, till my finger burns; then I lean in close and fix the tin eaves where the edges is bent down. Like it is now. Some of the colored younguns is most likely been standing on the porch, holding to eaves and swinging to the yard. I redo the doorsteps too, to where they ain't plumb even. And I figger I pro'bly been guilty of the same thing on the whole picture, making everything look too perfect.

I stop and scratch my head; my shadow does it too. Looks like some crazy from the insane asylum.

It's gone be dust-dark before I can go back and fix the other houses in the picture the way they really are. I can see them all in my head, backing up, what's wrong with them: no rotting porch posts, no loose shingles, no warped boards. The chimleys will be straight, no junk in the yards, no mangy dogs or mud holes. The yards ain't level like I drawed them.

I get mad with myself. I start to look back over the whole picture while I got a little light left, but I don't, won't give myself the satisfaction. I don't deserve it. Besides, I know I'm gone hate the whole thing, perfect like it is, a storybook town.

Buck's right: I am lazy. Laying down sleeping when I oughta been checking over my slubbering. I kick at the trash under my feet. Paper goes flying and dust squiggles drift in the orange shaft of sun, making the air show up. Air ain't clear neither. How could I draw air? That eats at me. I'm freezing to death. If I put off till tomorrow to fix what I've messed up today, I might lose interest. But my pencil and the light's just about give out.

Loujean

        — — — — — — — — — **S**ugar," says Miss Tissie, "before I go, I want to get a little cutting of your mama's sultana. See if I can't get it to root in water."

"Yes um," I say, "you go right ahead." I look down the line of chairs along the walls to see if I can locate the baby in one of the ladies' laps. Last time I seen her she was sleeping while they passed her around.

Miss Tissie wanders over to the plant stand in the northwest corner of the room and pinches out the whole top of Mama's sultana. I hope that's a sign she's leaving. She can take the whole pot, just go. I've had the toothache since ten this morning; it's five in the evening now, and the hurting ain't let up. I always time it to see if it's getting worse than it was before. It is.

The room looks strange, rust-stained from the setting sun, and everybody that's been here since right after dinner is beginning to look like they been here forever. But one thing they ain't is talked-out. Sounds like a room full of clapping hands. I prechate them coming, but I'm wore out and ashamed: Mama's body ain't ready, and here we are having a regular wake. I get my English composition book from the chest by my bed, rip out the notes, and throw them in the stove, then open the book to a clean sheet and put it on the mantelshelf of the boarded-up fireplace with a pencil for the ladies to put down what food they brung, in which dishes. The book on the mantelshelf makes the wake seem more real and respectable, and I feel easier knowing I won't get the dishes mixed up when it comes time to tote them home to the ladies after the funeral. There's the problem—I don't know if we'll be having a funeral.

Right now, I've got my hopes up. Aunt Annie Bell (she told me to call her "Anna Bell" from now on) and Aunt Rosanne is gone to the funeral home. Let's hope they've got the kind of money they make like they do and can set things right with the undertaker. I can tell everybody here's counting on them too.

My aunts showed up this morning in a long black shiny car, dressed for the funeral. High heels like tomwalkers; silky frocks tussling with corsets of cased flab; perfume canceling the snuffy-rust smell of the Scurvys; diamonds twinkling from my aunts' ears, down; even fur stoles bunched around their necks. I don't know where they're mink or not, but I know we're s'posed to think so.

Aunt Annie Bell strutted in first with her air cut off by her heavy-duty brassiere. Looked like all of her body doings—heart, liver, and lungs—was in her bosom, straining against the top of her tight frock. A big diamond on a gold chain jumping at her toady throat, she dabbed at her watery blue eyes with a white lace handkerchief balled up in a decorated fist—the biggest diamond ring you ever seen, but a little yellow. Her long nails was blood-red and sharp. Her heavy blond curls looked like they'd been varnished. She's from Etlanna. A secretary for the GBI.

Right in behind her, Aunt Rosanne, from New Orleans, come trolloping in, hollering at the old man eating his dinner. Big-built too, but broader-shouldered and standing a head higher than Aunt Annie Bell. But then her hair was a foot high, smut black and stretched up in a pile on top. Looked like a man in a wig to me. Weighted down in diamonds, just like Aunt Annie Bell: long dangly earbobs, a clustered diamond pin at her throat, rattley bracelets up to her elbows. Wide-painted mouth, and eyes so black and hard they looked like she drawed them with her eyebrow pencil.

My aunts scared me. Both of them ripping and raring—city cussing sounds worse than country cussing and means just what it says. Right off, the old man blurted out the problem about Mama. I don't think that was a good idear, not right off the bat like that. But, who knows, it might of been the best thing. Cause they couldn't wait to take off to the funeral home, hadn't never heard tell of no such a-thing, they said. I figger they must have at least heard of such things since they was raised around here.

I hadn't never laid eyes on Aunt Rosanne, but I'd been around Aunt Annie Bell once. Both of 'em together's something new. Who called them up is a myst'ry to me. Unless it was Buster. Aunt Ida Mae wouldn't have; she don't even speak to their type. Not that none of us is ever had the opportunity to run up on that type of women before. When Sonia Lee drug up around Cornerville last fall, we all thought we'd seen everything. She's a good bit older than me, but somehow she ended up in my room at school. Didn't last a week since the teacher wouldn't let her smoke in class. At recess, she'd hang out with the boys around the smoking tree, and the other girls would accuse their boyfriends of flirting with her. Now, up next to my aunts, Sonia Lee seems almost like one of us. At least, to my beknowest, she ain't carrying on about who's gone end up with the baby.

"Poor orphan child," said Aunt Annie Bell, scooping Joy up and smothering her to her hiked-up breasts. "What shall we do with you?" She clicked her tongue on the roof of her mouth: *"Nck nck nck!"*

"Don't look at me," Aunt Rosanne said. "I know I can't take her." Her penciled-on eyebrows shot up to just below her hairline, where it looked like the hair had been stitched to the scalp.

"We'll just have to make some arrangements." Aunt Annie Bell handed the baby back to me and picked the blanket lint off her black sleeve. *"Nck nck nck!"*

I hoped "some arrangements"—plural—meant they'd be talking business with the undertaker. I'd gladly put up with them till after the funeral, then let them know the baby stays here.

Prancing back in from the funeral home, they are starving slap to death. They speak high-and-mighty to the church ladies, to kin they don't claim, to the rest of our neighbors, then shove on through the crowd to the eating table, piling food on their plates from the tinfoil-covered bowls and platters—a little dab of everything.

The ladies in the kitchen, warming up and putting

away the food, picking ice in the dishpan, hurry into the living room with glasses of iced tea for my aunts. Same as they do for everybody else, but they do gaze a little longer at my aunts, like they're movie stars. Looks like my aunts expect it too.

Aunt Rosanne wants coffee now, and somebody bustles off to get her a cup. Aunt Annie Bell changes her mind, will have coffee instead of tea "to take the chill off."

I feel kind of proud of my aunts, but ashamed too: proud, because I've got so little else to be proud of and need it so bad now, since Mama ain't here for the wake. They do add a sparkle to the drab room, as out of place as they look, like poodles running with fice dogs. But I'm ashamed of how they act so important. Sticking their noses up in the air, talking sweet cause they're hungry, but treating the ladies like hired help.

My teeth are still hurting—all of them.

I notice my aunts are happiest when they're eating. They eat pretty, with good manners, but eat a long time and lots. Then they get miserable, take off their high heels and slouch around in their black stockings on the floor that ain't none too clean.

Standing in the trail of bark and splinters from the window to the stove, Aunt Rosanne picks a splinter out of the toe of her left stocking and holds it up to the orangy light of the window, studying it like some strange bug. I wish I'd had the guts to go on and ask them if they fixed everything up—if they made the "arrangements"—at the funeral home before they got full and cross. Now, I'll just have to hope. Besides, the hand-clapping sound of talking is so thick I pro'bly couldn't get a word in edgewise.

The old man's kin is still straggling in: tight-lipped, timid, drooped. A fat baby on every girl's hip. Even the women smoke, dip, or chew. Skint-head boy cousins, who will go from being roosters to troublemakers to down-and-out old men trailing cross-armed behind religious wifes, without ever setting foot outside of Swanoochee County.

Scurvys ain't well thought of. Kind of trashy. But they been in Swanoochee County since they was a Swanoochee County, since dirt, and are best thought of for keeping to theirselfs.

Cousin Undine starts: "I recollect how Aunt Imer used to drive Great-Uncle John in from the flatwoods to the courthouse during the Great Depression. . . ."

I don't have to listen, I know the story by heart. Old Man's told it a million times, a million ways. Telling it in Scurvy talk—a's and o's muffled into r's by their thick tongues—about the Great Depression and Great-Uncle John coming in, in his big car, in his big hat, to give the county a big bunch of money to keep going on. And didn't that entitle every Scurvy from now till the Rapture to a check—welfare—which they never claim to draw but do? Even as to the old man, who would have a stroke if you mentioned it.

Great-Uncle John knowed us well: leaving his money to the county for us to draw on in time of need, expecting we might sorry away anyhow, being the kind of people who'd throw his money away in one clip if he'd left it to us straight out. We're welfare people, for a fact. I don't want to be like the other Scurvys—us—but I don't know as I've got it in me to be no other way but.

I see Aunt Annie Bell taking over two spaces on the

couch, and Miss Joyce, beside her, get up and amble off to the kitchen to take her turn at doing the dishes being paraded from table to dishpan and back.

The water pipes is thawed out, and now I got to remember to leave the spigots dripping tonight. And on top of everything else, the firewood's running low.

Where is Buck and them?

It ain't all that cold in here, what with everybody stirring about—talking, eating, laughing, and crying. Aunt Rosanne starts crying first and sets off some of the other ladies (she's rocking in the old man's chair, like Queen-for-a-Day, and I know if he catches her, she'll find out she ain't).

"Our poor lil ole sister," she says to the women leant over her, hugging her neck.

I pull the chain on the light overhead to get rid of the orangy light of sundown that's been making me feel like time's standing still, and the white light showering down on me makes me feel like the night's just getting started, won't be over for a long time, but won't last near long enough before it's time for the funeral, which I don't know if we're even gone be having. Through the huddle of ladies in the middle of the room, I catch sight of the baby's pink blanket. It's time for her to eat. I wonder if she's cold. I decide to go on and put the last piece of wood on the fire and then go heat up her bottle. I hope nobody ain't messed with the formula in the Frigidaire. How many times have I heard that door screel open and slap shut?

I go to the end of the couch, where Aunt Annie Bell's setting, rared back so she can breathe. Her black-stockinged legs are stuck out, blocking the walking space between the couch and the table. Long crooked toes, stockings smelling like scorch. "Excuse me, Aunt Annie Bell." I have to reach around her varnished blond head to get to the window over the wood scaffold.

"Anna Bell," she says.

"Anna Bell," I say.

"You're excused," she says and leans forward.

I wind the curtain and tuck it between her stuffed back and the couch, and when I look out the window, I see Earl grinning over a stack of firewood on the scaffold. His nose and ears is red; his cap bill is turned around, making his broad white forehead look broader. He's wearing his brown-plaid shirt, the one he generally wears when he's working or waiting to go to work: toe-tapping and popping his knuckles, trailing after me like I'm a she-dog in heat.

He pokes a stick of firewood through the busted window pane.

"Thank you," I say, taking it, hating to leave the window, the seeping cold air, the split-oak smell, the white trees on the creek, the freedom and peace of the still, framed dusk. I hate to leave the surprise face: Earl. "I took care of that busted pipe under the house," he says, reaching down and picking up another piece of firewood, placing it on the scaffold, building a wall between us, a wall over my only lookout.

He always overdoes everything. Now, I'm closed in with the white light and jabbering.

"Such coarse children," Aunt Annie Bell says to one of the ladies setting beside her on the couch. Then to me as I turn around, "Where's your father?" She grabs my free hand and rubs it between hers like she's figgering on me for some project.

"He's out . . . making arrangements," I say and smile. Now I can ask her. I bend down close, smelling her nylony doll hair, and whisper in her diamond-weighted ear. "Did everything go okay at the funeral home?"

Straining up to my ear, with one hand on the back of my neck tugging me closer, she whispers, "That old son-ofabitch!"

Is she talking about the old man? the undertaker? Did she tell him off? pay him? promise him? Walking toward the stove with the firewood, I watch her head tilt back on the couch, her eyes close. Blue shadow on the lids make them look open. Her pink lipstick's zigzagged like rickrack. Her rouged cheeks go slack. I know a look of pain, and I know a look of being whipped. And that's not pain on her face.

My aunts don't have no money, I decide. Maybe just enough to keep theirselfs gussied up and putting on airs, enough for a fine car to come home in and make like the girls that went away and made something out of theirselfs. But not enough money for a funeral. My heart aches like my teeth. Unless Buck or somebody does the "arranging," we won't be having no funeral. I know it like I know the sun will come up in the morning, just don't know where it'll shine or not cause of clouds.

It's too hot in here now. I feel like I'm fixing to faint. My stomach is gnawing from smelling coffee. I need to tell everybody the truth. I can't yet. They're still bringing in food, coming to set up all night. I need to throw up, but don't have time. The baby's crying, lost in the crowd.

Soon she's being passed along a chain of women, all of them cooing and kissing her on the head, till she gets to me.

When I think things can't get no worse, Sonia Lee pops in. Just opens the door and slips through like a cat and stands behind the old man's chair. Straight blond hair down to her butt, wild eyes stretched like she's hunting a rat.

If them two fat aunts of mine knowed what I know, they'd be hiding their diamonds and fur stoles, stead of flaunting them. One of them's fur stole is hanging like a squirrel over the back of the old man's chair, where Sonia Lee is staked out. Must be Aunt Rosanne's since Aunt Annie Bell, setting on the couch, is got hers laying across her lap.

I go get the baby's suck bottle—one of the ladies has warmed it up. Bowls and pans, in tinfoil tents, all over the cook table and stove in the little slip of a kitchen off the living room. The foil catches the naked light from the bulb overhead. The kitchen's the cleanest I ever seen it, smells like bleach and stings my eyes. I wish I could go out in the cold air for a minute. I like the creek at dust-dark, the way it flows in chilly whispers. Maybe Sonia Lee will be gone when I look again. Things seemed so respectable before. Now she's part of my shame. I dread the old man coming in, him and the boys. I'm ashamed of them all. My face feels white; light on the tinfoil, white; the room, white; the baby, a live coal in my hands, her bawling mouth making no sound, just my ears ringing, hot white.

Somebody sets a chair behind me for me to set down and feed the baby. I hope nobody don't announce that I'm about to faint, since then they'll all crowd around me. Maybe they can't tell yet. What if I drop the baby?

Through the kitchen door, I see Sonia Lee still staked out behind the old man's chair. She looks like she's mildewed. My eyes suck back in my head. I'm even ashamed to faint. I can't faint. Thinking that makes the sparkles and speckles begin to fade. I can see clear again, hear again, and find out I was just as well off fixing to faint.

The racket's awful. Sonia Lee will leave in a minute when she finds out the old man and the boys ain't coming in, I promise myself. But I figger if they happen up on this crowd, they'll take off. They'd run a risk of freezing slap to death by sleeping in the courthouse breezeway before they'd face such a fine crowd. I feel jealous of them.

Aunt Annie Bell hangs in the kitchen door, rasping the top of one stockinged foot with the sole of the other, and addresses the church ladies: "Would one of y'all please be a sweetheart and cut me a slice of that chocolate cake?"

Buck

After losing the old man on the Swanoochee, I decide to make myself scarce around Cornerville—keep driving the forking dirt roads through the flatwoods—till dark. Ain't all that worried about the old man; figger he'll come out somewheres around the Florida line when he's good and ready, then hike up 129 to the house. This business with Buster—running shine—is what's worrying me.

You can tell a born rogue from one that ain't. Buster's meanness is right out in the open. He ain't out riding and shaking like me, you can count on that. He's right there where he always is with his feet under Aunt Ida's eating table, or prowling about Cornerville. Me, I'm dreading nightfall, fretting myself into believing the law's done after me with a load of shine. The longest waiting I ever done in my life. I got it all down good in my mind, every step of the plan, and I know it ain't gone come out nowheres close.

Long about seven o'clock, I head south through the flatwoods, then after another mile of gallberries and palmettos, and my second Goody headache powder for the day, I turn west on the dirt straightaway by the Florida line. Shore enough, I see the old man's tracks in the white sand leading out toward 129. I'd laugh if I wadn't so scared and tight in the chest. Old Man can natural take care of hisself! Again, I feel proud—he's got that tough Injun blood running in his veins. I feel like ain't nery bit of it running in mine. Chicken blood's what I got. But I'm going through with this business with Buster, come hell or high water.

The tall pines either side of the road looks like they been punched out of the cold gray sky to a black backing. A flock of coots fly over with their wings whipping the still air. They light in a slew where straggling cypress trees touch the evening star. The old man's tracks go on.

Getting close to 129, smack dab on the Georgia-Florida line, I can see The Line's lights through the barred windows of the cinder-block building. Three pickups parked out front. Old Man's tracks veer right, petering out at the grass ditch. I set there a minute, with the post truck engine hassling like a overheated dog, and gaze north up the pewter highway, the dark ditch, trying to pick him out in the tunnel of pines. Nothing. I ease on across the highway to The Line and stop on the shoulder, switch off the truck, and get out. I don't once think Pee Wee might not be in there. Thinking's about the worst thing I can do, what I've tried all evening not to do, not to plan it all out, reasonable and heartless, cause if I think too much I won't go with Buster. Getting Pee Wee into it's about as low as I can go. Makes me want to ditch the whole thing, but if I do Mama'll stay right where she is. I step through the screen door—plastic over wire—to the red light of the square room. A pinball machine on the left wall, two fellers playing. Another one setting at the bar, facing the door, don't know he's on the place. Pee Wee setting where he always sets, at the north end of the bar, with one beer left from each six-pack he's done drunk. They's two beer and a tore-open carton of beer before him, so I know he's on his third six-pack. Which means he's gone be easier to handle. One six-pack, he'll fight you. Over two and he's normally like a little youngun, don't much care where he's going, long as he's going. I hate myself.

"He ain't paid for that last one," says Solder—sour-faced, bloated old man runs The Line now.

I give him two dollars and he gives me back some change.

"It's cold in here," I say.

"They better off that way." He steps up to the cash register and punches the keys. The bell rings like a boxing match is fixing to start.

I help Pee Wee gather up his beer by punching the two leftover cans into the open end of the six-pack he's drinking on. They just fit, but he has trouble keeping the loose end up. I try to help him and he thinks I'm trying to steal his beer.

"Come on, Bubber," I say—we all call him Bubber when he gets like this, treat him pitiful and helpless. He is. I wonder if we was to play like we didn't even know him if he wouldn't straighten up. He wouldn't. Right now, I don't want to think of him pitiful, just mean and aggravating. Thinking like that helps with what I gotta do. "Take it your ownself then!" I say, shoving the beer at him.

Following me out, he staggers and mumbles and bumps the door jamb. His face is twisted; his mouth is slack. Looks like he's fixing to go to fighting. I'm glad of it.

"One day I ain't gone come after you, boy!" I say.

"Y'all don't leave him here on me," calls Solder.

"Go to hell, you sonofabitch!" Pee Wee starts back in.

I turn him around into the cold night air.

"Shit!" he says, hugging his beer, and then says to me, "Don't tell the old man I been cussing," and cackles.

Out in the open he smells ranker, like he's been sick on hisself. I go to stuff him in the truck and a can of beer drops to the gravel and rolls under the truck. I bend down to pick it up and he bails out and grabs me from behind. We go to tussling.

"Stop it now," I say, and for a skinny drunk he's got me pretty good. Arms pinned to my sides. I could throw him if I was a mind to, but I feel too guilty about what I'm fixing to get him into. So we scuffle out to the highway, then back to the front of the truck, like we're dancing. His breath, coming over my shoulder, is like buzzard bait.

He spots the beer where it's rolled to the front bumper, turns me loose, and gets down on his hands and knees and paws it. I help him up and in the truck again like nothing ain't never happened. God, he's a mess! I crank up and feel the blood beating in my head, my heart knocking against my ribcage. My eyeballs is dried out so bad I can't hardly see from driving all evening with the truck heater on. I know it's gone get worser before the night's over but I don't see how.

He's study drinking and smoking, trying to set hisself afire. Still driving, north up 129, I fumble around and beat out his britches and he takes a lick at me. Long about halfway to Cornerville, I see the old man making time along the shoulder of frostbit grass, him and the grass both the color of dried corn shucks. Walking with his elbows cocked. I drive on past, cuss myself, back up, and lean across Pee Wee, rolling the window down.

"You want a lift, Old Man?" I holler.

"You!" hollers the old man. "You S.B.!" He shakes his finger at me and trots off down the ditch.

"Old Man, I wadn't trying to steal your fishing hole," I holler back.

Pee Wee yells, "Sonofabitch—just say it, Old Man," and conks me on the head with his beer can, and I see stars about the same time I see headlights speeding up the road behind me. I take off like Moody's goose, looking in the rearview mirror—could be the law. A white car comes on around the post truck, tires singing on the gravel. My face goes hot and cold. I'm getting as edgy as a widder woman. The light at the crossing in Cornerville's been set to blink on red, and from a mile away, I start worrying about it being a roadblock.

"Hell, I ain't even done nothing yet," I say out loud, and Pee Wee says, "You ain't telling me nothing." Passing the café, I see Alamand through the front window playing the pinball machine. And up ahead is Buster's pickup parked in front of the courthouse, this side of the telephone booth. He's got it running, smoke puffing from the tail pipe and scooting along the sidewalk. I pull up behind him and shut off, figgering I'm gone have a time getting Pee Wee out and loaded on the back of Buster's truck. Some strange lard-ass woman's talking on the phone in the phone booth, don't even turn to look.

I've done made up my mind to go tell Buster if he wants Pee Wee to come get him, figgering Pee Wee'll put up such a fuss that Buster'll leave him setting where he is, and we can go on without him. I start to take the keys out of the truck, but don't—just in case I don't come back, in case I go to the pen or get killed one, and the boys might need the truck to make a living with. They can always go back in the carpentering business, building outhouses cheap. But they's always something: we bout got sued for the one we took the most pains building for Locust Road Church across the river. Claimed we used rotten lumber. Won't no lumber hold up two big fat deacons at one time. Reckon how many times you got to tell these people that two holes in one bench won't work?

I get out to go tell Buster to come get Pee Wee if he wants him, and Pee Wee wallers out the other side with his beer and follows me like a dog for the first time in his life.

"Load up!" Buster yells out his truck window.

I duck under the camper top and set down on the labor bench, right side, hoping Pee Wee might balk, but he piles on in and sets down facing me. It's dark as all get-out in here. Outside, on the courtyard grass, two lights is shining up on the brick wall where it says SWANOOCHEE COUNTY COURTHOUSE in chrome lettering. I can smell pine tar and all kinds of slop—axle grease, chew tobacco, deer tongue—but I can't see my hand in front of my face. Pee Wee pops the top of a beer can—*poop*!

Bout the time Buster puts the truck in gear and starts to take off, Alamand comes ambling up around the back of the post truck, peeps inside, then looks at Buster's truck. I get still and lean against the wall.

"Get your ass in here!" hollers Pee Wee, just as Buster eases out on the highway. "We gotta go to work."

Alamand looks addled, skips a little, then chases after Buster's truck, latches onto the camper, and swings in. Pee Wee slips over so he can set down, looking dumb with his hands between his knees. Buster makes a left onto 94, at the red light, and I can see people wandering in and out the front of our house, a big black Buick parked on the cement slope. At first I think it's a hearse. I start to bail out, but then I see it's a regular car and wonder who it could be. Can't come up with nobody I know of owning no car like that.

Buster's moving on now, past the rows of houses each side of the hardroad, past the cemetery, where the tomb-stones gives off a white glow, and then the Alapaha River bridge. A tire tool flams on the floor, Pee Wee and Alamand shuffle and mumble. And I can just make out Alamand's set white face with a pink coloration from the taillights. I don't say nothing, feel like I'm froze, and figger Buster's picked up a nigger or two from the quarters to help load the shine, because Pee Wee's moved to the cab wall of the truck, talking to somebody else. I wonder who Buster's got indebted to him but don't really care all that much. I got my hands full. Pee Wee's subject to get us all killed with his mouth, and now I gotta babysit Alamand.

"I swear!" I say, throwing my head back against the cold metal wall of the camper top.

We go on a piece and then Buster slows down, turns on his left blinker and heads south down the old Jennings–Lake Park road. Nothing but woods all around us, the blood-red gravel behind us scabbing over the deeper we get in the woods. Now and again, lights from houses shines through the trees. I know them all: the Peterson old place, the Crawford old place, the Herring old place. That's it. From here on to Jennings, Florida—if that's where we going—it's just me and a bunch of babies and a rattlesnake in the lonesomest stretch of west Swanoochee County.

Buster the rattlesnake turns off at last down a three-path buggy road and don't even bother with making shore he don't kill the help, knocking our heads together with his driving. Cutting back and to and around curves, scrub oaks and pine limbs beating at the top and sides of the camper top like a bad storm.

Of a sudden, he stops, and we all pile up at the cab—beer cans rolling, Pee Wee cussing, Alamand grunting, and somebody breathing hard—in a knot and go to untangling.

Buster leaves the engine running, gets out, and struts around to the back. He's bright pink from the taillights, wet-blond hair and all, and his eyes and nose and mouth looks sunk in, his face like the devil's. "Y'all can unload now, boys," he says. "Come on."

Cold smoke's shooting out his nose and mouth, out the tail pipe. All of us looks like we're smoking, it's so cold. He steps back and I bail out, Alamand right in behind me. He ain't said nery word till yet, but I can tell by the way he's scratching his head he knows we ain't gone be cutting no fence posts or putting up outhouses. I wish I could look that dumb and make the rest of the world wait on me.

Pee Wee comes out cussing and rubbing his head with a cigarette singeing his hair. "I be a sonofabitch," he says, hopping off the back of the truck. He stumbles, falls.

Buster helps him up and brushes him off, and he just moseys off to the bushes and starts unzipping and peeing at the same time.

"Take your time, boys," Buster says, crossing his arms and grinning. "We got all night."

"Where's the car?" I say to Buster, looking back to see who's easing down off the tailgate. I can't believe my eyes. "Earl!" I say.

"How you, Buck?" He grins and rams his hands in his pockets, rattling change.

"What the hell?" I say, this time to Buster.

"I done stole some of your post help, Scooter." Buster teehees in his hand. "Done stole some of his post help," he says again, like he's saying it to somebody off there in the bushes. He'll do that when he gets one on you.

"How come, Earl?" I say.

He shrugs, shame-faced, toeing at the dirt with his hardened brogans. I don't know why I don't want him here—maybe cause I don't need another baby to tend to in that car doing ninety-to-nothing with a load of shine—but I think I don't want him here cause he's too good for this. I don't want him ruint like the rest of us. Bad as he's been to take up with whatever meanness we get into, he ain't never messed with no shine. Maybe I know, deep down, if they's anybody can be depended on to look out for Loujean and the baby, it's Earl.

"Here they come," Buster says, "right on the money."

He swaggers off down the dark buggy path toward two headlights and a thundering rumble coming straight on. Sounds like a big transfer truck, and from the looks of the other lights framing the body through the thick trees, I can tell it's a good-size truck. I didn't expect Buster would bring us straight to the shine still or the car; he's about got plans to ship us out in that truck and let whoever's doing the driving take us to the next stop. If somebody gets caught, it ain't gone be Buster. He keeps his hands clean. Specially outside of Swanoochee County, where he's a nobody like the rest of us.

The truck stops about twenty-five yards off and we're all listening, scared stiff. Earl's still kicking around the truck, out of the light. Alamand's bent over on the tailgate like he's puking. Pee Wee's back, smoking, with his pants unzipped and twisted. He's got one hip cocked like he's hitchhiking on the highway.

"What we doing here, Buck?" Alamand says, his voice going off inside the camper. Earl slaps his shoulder, hangs his hand there, then walks off. He looks solid and honest in his plaid work shirt. Looks like he's dressed to save his good clothes and give a honest man a honest day's work: Earl.

I hear Buster talking to the driver of the big truck, a low scattering mumble across the dark woods. Then he hollers out, "Y'all get on over here, boys!"

I look at Earl; he looks at me. I know he's smart, real smart, smarter than ery one of us, even if he does act dumb. I want to ask him again how come.

"How come, Earl?" I say.

"Because," he says and walks off toward the transfer truck with us all following.

I know he's got a good reason. His being serious for once blows my mind. I wish he would cut up or stump his toe and act silly. I can see his blocky back in the dark, hear his shoes scraping bear grass, briers snagging his pants. I wish they all would take off through the woods; I wish the moon in the west would grow round from that little white slice.

"Y'all boys come on," Buster calls out and laughs. "Y'all's ride's waiting."

"We're coming," Earl hollers.

"I hear you," says Buster, laughs. Earl's the leader now; I'm following. I can hear Alamand clearing his throat behind me; Pee Wee, behind him, blowing his nose. When we get up to the transfer, the headlights blinds us and I can't make out who's doing the driving, just a thick white arm propped in the window, burnt diesel fogging the clear, cold air.

Buster's standing by the driver's side, propping on the door with his feet crossed, jabbering.

"Load up, boys," he says, nodding toward the back of the idling truck, and goes to talking to the driver again. Sounds like he's speaking in tongues.

Earl loads up first, feeling his way in along the cold metal walls to where a bunch more boys is standing and squatting. No talking, just hard breathing. I come in behind Earl, looking back to make shore Alamand and Pee Wee gets in. Pee Wee bellies up and stands on the edge, holding to a hank of rope dangling from the top.

From the dark front end of the truck body, squeezed between Alamand and Earl, warming in the heat of everybody hassling, I watch Pee Wee. Braced with his left foot out, he looks like a play soldier. Stone sober. Used to loading up to pull out. He don't look brave, just used to it and mad.

Loujean

————————I'm just getting the baby down for the night when I hear the old man coming through the back door. She's wore out from being passed about all evening, sweet as pie when she's sleeping like this. Her head looks like a ripe peach. I kiss it and it smells like one too. I wonder if I've spoilt her already and her not but three days old.

In the kitchen, I can hear the ladies speaking to the old man, kind of standoffish. I know he's a sight for sore eyes before I look back through the kitchen door. I can't believe he's come in with them all here. He's making over them, hugging necks, everlast one of them. All except for Aunt Rosanne and Aunt Annie Bell, who ain't making no move toward him neither. Aunt Annie Bell's rared back again on the couch with her arms rolled in her fur stole. Her eyes is closed; I know she's not asleep cause I see her purple eyelids twitching. Aunt Rosanne's setting with her ankles crossed in his chair by the front door. I wish she'd move somewheres else, cause he's looking hard at her and is liable to walk over and dump her.

Sonia Lee's still staked out behind his chair, with one hand on Aunt Rosanne's fur stole across the back. She's blowing smoke over Aunt Rosanne's chimley stack of hair. Nobody ain't made a move to go home, and it's got to be going on eleven o'clock. I can't see the clock on the mantelshelf for ladies lined up in front of it. They're waiting. I know for what. But I still ain't got the heart to say Mama's corpse ain't coming home, they ain't gone be no funeral. I been thinking about a memorial service (I've seen that done on TV), but it don't seem like something would work around Cornerville.

The old man's setting down at the eating table, fixing to eat from a plate piled high with food one of the ladies brung him. He's got his elbows on the table, two caked streaks of blood from his nose to his mouth, like cracked red paint. His thin gray hair's sticking up on top, his baggy britches is muddy and tore on one knee. He goes to eating like he's starved to death while everybody talks and watches him. I wish I could say he looks like that cause he's been out working—they's honor in that.

"Thankee, ma'am," he says when one of the ladies hands him a fruit jar of tea. He takes it by the rim, guzzles it down, shakes the ice, and one of them takes it back and fills it up again.

Three mean old boy-cousins bust in the front door, plowing through the crowd in the living room and kitchen, and out the back door with a streak of cold air chasing after them.

"You boys settle down now," Aunt Undine says about a minute too late. She slides to the edge of her chair, stands up, and waddles to the front door, spits out, and shuts it.

The old man's grinning with his gums shining, eyeballing the path where the boys plowed through. Uncle Albert hikes his britches and moseys over to the eating table and sets down by the old man. He rocks his chair closer, studying the old man's face. "I was shore sorry to hear about hit," Uncle Albert says. His sun-tough face is wrinkled like a wadded paper sack.

Still gumming his food, the old man reaches over and slaps Uncle Albert on the shoulder.

Somebody slams the back door. More food.

"Mr. Lay," Miss Amaretta says to the old man, "you want some coffee?"

"No um, this is fine, fine." He swigs from his tea jar again, rattles the ice. She hurries over with a tea pitcher and fills it again. Looks like the Virgin Mary in her blue cotton frock and white hair, the holiest person I ever seen. He's checking her out with his nickel-plated green eyes. His beaten face is one big grin.

Tilting back now, he looks like he's mulling over Aunt Rosanne in his chair, who ain't took her eyes off him since he come in. I figger he's getting full and wants to set there and catch a nap. He always naps, even at night. But before long, I see he's got his eyes on Sonia Lee behind his chair. Just looking at her while he eats, like he's dreaming about her and his mind has conjured her stroking that mink stole like she's trying to tame it.

She won't go on as long as he's got a dime in his pockets. I know that. Normally, I'd take the risk of trying to run her off, but not in front of company. When he gets done eating, they'll likely leave together. Let 'em. He ain't shaming Mama and us no more than he ever has. Sonia

Lee's brown eyes squeeze light as she blows smoke straight at him like a signal. He's grinning, gumming on a biscuit clutched in one fist like a idiot.

I know he really wants his chair now.

"Y'all done took care of everything?" he asks Aunt Rosanne, who has murder in her eye.

Aunt Annie Bell sets up straight on the couch. "What's it to you?" she says.

"Don't talk to him," says Aunt Rosanne, locking her ringed fingers on her lap.

Sonia Lee blows another stream of smoke over her head.

"Get off my back, gal!" Aunt Rosanne says and turns, staring at her.

Sonia Lee don't move a hair; one corner of her rind mouth twitches. You can hear a pin drop, the clock ticking like it's just been rewound.

"Miss Amaretta," I say, "did you put down who brung that banana pudding?" I wade right in amongst them all to the mantelshelf and start looking over the long list of names and dishes in my composition book.

"Seems like I did, sugar," she says. "Let me see."

She stands so close I can smell her warm vanilla cooking on her, and I know she's caught on I'm ashamed, but I like having her there. She don't take no pleasure in nobody's pain. Like some I could name.

"How come the old lady ain't been brung home yet?" The old man stands up, holding his bowed back.

"How come you haven't done something about it?" Aunt Annie Bell, on the end of the couch by the mantelshelf, holds the tail of my dress to one side so she can see him.

Old Man's heating up. "If y'all hain't come to see to the old lady's funeral," he says, "how come you here?"

I just stand there, looking at the list and Miss Amaretta's clean-cut fingernails.

She turns, facing the old man, and wipes her hands on her white apron. "Don't you worry, Mr. Lay. We're gone take up a collection in church, first thing tomorrow morning."

"Prechate it, ma'am," he says, but keeps his eyes on Aunt Rosanne in his chair, on Sonia Lee.

Sonia Lee can stand in one place longer than anybody. Looks like finally she's enjoying herself.

"I'll have you know," says Aunt Annie Bell, squirming to the edge of the couch and speaking to Miss Amaretta through the old man, "my little sister is no charity case."

Miss Amaretta stares at her, her soft gray eyes going hard. I ain't never seen this side of her, and I think how maybe they's two sides to everybody.

"That hain't charity!" pipes the old man.

Aunt Rosanne scrambles to her feet. "What is it then, Lay Scurvy?"

"Church business," he says.

"Church business?" Aunt Annie Bell grunts herself up.

"Hit's shore hard times," says Uncle Albert, shaking his head. "Buster's fault," blurts Aunt Undine. She wallows up from her chair, hands braced on her blocky hips, and starts parading, giving off whiffs of snuff and that famous Scurvy self-pity.

As Aunt Undine paces past the old man's chair, Sonia Lee puffs smoke down Aunt Rosanne's chimley stack of hair.

"I *said*, quit blowing smoke in my hair." Aunt Rosanne bats at her horns of smoke. "The idea!"

Oh, Lord! One thing's about as good as another; I'd just as soon they quarrel over Buster.

Aunt Annie Bell stands, giant-size with her pumped-up bosom and girdled fat, and gets loud. "You was counting on us, weren't you, Lay Scurvy?" The light overhead sets off a confusion of sparkles from her earbobs and rings and the tinfoil-tented dishes on the table.

"Set down, you old toady frog!" says the old man. "Before I pop your jaws."

"Just do it, fellow," she says, toddling toward him, "and I'll call the law on you so fast."

Neither one of my aunts don't seem classy now, and everything's out in the open. I feel naked.

"They ain't gone be no funeral," I announce, stepping ahead of Aunt Annie Bell and facing everybody. "I prechate y'all coming and bringing stuff and helping out, but you can go on home now." Feels like the words is coming out of somebody else's mouth.

"Of course there will be, honey," says Miss Amaretta, moving from the mantelshelf to where I stand. "You'll see." She hugs me and I watch while the old man fishes in his pockets and pulls out a rolled strand of haywire. Slump-shouldered, he strolls over and hangs it on a nail drove in the wall next to his chair, then sidles behind Aunt Rosanne, who is still standing, puffed-up and mean, and sits in his own chair.

"*Nck nck nck!*" she says. "What my baby sister's had to put up with!"

I don't cry nor nothing, but the baby does. I go over

and scoop her out of the dresser drawer and lay her squalling on the bed. When I look back, ain't nobody made a move to go home. They're all quiet and still, the light glinting off the tinfoil on the table. The clock ticking. Almost midnight.

My kin people on the old man's side acts like nothing ain't happened, like they're here for the duration and everybody's fussing over nothing: people get born, they suffer, they die. Up to God and the county to see to the rest of it. Aunt Undine parades from the kitchen to the living room, from the living room to the kitchen.

Aunt Rosanne plops down in the old man's chair again.

I look closer. Is she sitting in the old man's lap? No. He's gone. Sonia Lee is gone. Aunt Rosanne's fur stole is gone.

"Will one of y'all put another piece of wood on the fire?" I say.

The baby's wet and cold, and I'm burning up again.

Old Man

Sonia Lee stands on the boardwalk, gazing out at the Troublesome Creek dip, sunk in the dark. Then she flops that fur wrop about her shoulders and prances off down the cement slope and around a big black car parked in front of the house. Looks like a million bucks with that long blond hair trapped under that wrop, the way hit pooches out at the neck. I can tell right now she hain't never gone be the kind to go hog wild over nothing I dig out of no dumpster.

"Old Man," she says—don't even look back, "you want to go riding with me?"

"Yeah, babe," I say. I could-a swore she didn't know I slipped out of the house behind her when she eased that fur wrop off the back of my chair.

She swings open the car door and gets in under the steering wheel. I don't know who the devil that car belongs to, but I reckon hit's hers now. She's setting gazing at me through the windshield with her chin on the steering wheel. The red light at the crossing blinks on the windows, puts me in mind of some big town I'm aiming to go to someday. I don't care which one, long as Sonia Lee's there. Deep down, I know I oughta be in the house, suffering, but I figger a little ride hain't gone hurt nobody. And if I get out of the way, maybe them old biddies will know they can't depend on me for no "arrangements." They got money, let them handle hit. Anybody with that much gall's bound to know how to make a trade with a undertaker.

I hain't getting into hit! Learn them boys how to take hold when I'm gone. "For their own sakes," I say out loud, knowing I'm a lie and just itching to get in that car.

Sonia Lee cranks up, and I hop down off the stoop and shag on out to the car and get in on the other side. I don't get the door shet good before she hits the gas, quick down the Troublesome Creek dip and due north on 129. My neck jerks and burns like I'm getting lectrocuted.

"This car can natural move!" I say.

She stares straight ahead, driving and smiling—something Sonia Lee don't generally do.

Flashing past the old Sampson Camp, to our left, they's a good twenty-odd houses with lights in the windows; we going so fast looks like one big house lit up. Camp's been shet down—used to make dynamite out of litard stumps in the flatwoods—but still's got people living there.

"Use to work for Sampson Powder Company," I say. She sets high, keeps driving. "Where we going, babe?" I say.

She's lighting up a cigarette, then turning the dial on the radio, music and jabbering and static running together. Wide open, the radio and the car. She stops turning and some man goes to sanging by hisself. I can't make no sense out of hit; I don't care. She picks up speed and I hang on to the door handle. I hain't scared, just worked up. She rolls the window down. The cold wind whipping at the wrop makes the fur riffle. Her brown eyes is squinched up, her pale round face is red pied.

Feels like the wheels is clearing the road. We're flying. Pinewoods on both sides of the road going to Withers, where I been a bunch of times. Hain't nothing but a old turpentine camp with a railroad track, some nigger quarters. If she goes straight north, we could wind up in Etlanna. I don't care if she do.

I'm freezing slap to death, but I don't let on. She goes to sanging and I hum along, us cutting through the cold like we trying to outrun hit. Etlanna—don't care if we do. I hain't never felt nothing like this; must be like what a bird feels flying. I don't give a fig if Sonia Lee don't never wait on me, that's what old women like Miss Amaretta is for. I'll take this life anytime, me and my babe cutting through the dark, following where the car lights takes us.

We streak up the hill on the railroad overpass, just south of Withers, and when we shoot down, my stomach jumps to my throat. She passes the turnoff to Withers and I figger for a fact we bound for Etlanna. Of a sudden, she slams the brakes and I shoot out of the seat and hit the dashboard with my nose. Brakes screeching, rubber burning, sharp black smoke pouring in the car. I've heared myself hit but don't feel nothing, just see her white hands a-turning the steering wheel, my ownself flopping around, saying, "Look out!"

She rams the car in reverse, and I look back just in time to see a big transfer truck tearing down off the overpass for the tail of the car. Headlights like shooting stars. "Look out!" I holler.

She guns the car west off 129 at the Withers turnoff, the back end sliding around into a row of mailboxes, cropping them off like matchsticks.

The truck tires screech and the driver lays down on the horn, goes on north.

I feel the blood from my nose running to my mouth. I don't say nothing, just hang on. She's picking up speed again, tooling past the lamp-lit nigger shacks each side of the hardroad, sanging. A old gyp dog comes yapping out from one of the yards and dodges around the wheels of the car. Sonia Lee jerks the car shoulder to shoulder, trying to miss hit, I guess. The dog chases us till we get out of Withers, gives up, and goes on back to the house.

The hardroad curves through close pines hung with bullous vines. I prop one foot on the dashboard and brace myself, seeing up ahead a cement bridge blaring in the headlights. When she gets to hit, she just stops. I set there, rocking. She opens up the door and gets out, still sanging the same song while some man on the radio's a-jabbering about Goodyear tires. White light inside. She strolls back and to, up and down the Alapaha River bridge, then steps up on the cement railing with her dirty white tennises shining, sanging and staring down with her arms out. That fur wrop like wings above her butt-slick dungarees.

I just set there with my foot on the dashboard, figgering she's subject to jump right back in and take off without me if I get out. Shore nuf, I see her hop backards off the railing, turn, and head for the car. She jumps in, slams the door, and takes off like a brim chasing a bass from its bed. This time I'm ready. You couldn't beat me out of this seat with a litard knot. Bout the time she picks up some speed again, she slows down and spins around on a white clay ramp and straightens up on the hardroad again.

I hain't for shore, but I think we're going back where we come from and I dread the overpass. I got both feet braced on the dashboard now, scrunched down with my neck bent back against the seat. I can't see over the dashboard. But when we go to clacking over the river bridge, I have to set up, see where I'm going. Can't stand not seeing what's fixing to be the end of us. When we get back to Withers, here comes that confounded dog, yapping around the wheels again.

Just like before, Sonia Lee goes to laughing and dodging the car shoulder to shoulder to keep from hitting the dog. I hain't moving nery hair, despite her snatching the car side to side. Headlights flashing on the shanties like she's shining coons in persimmon trees. We're coming up on the fork of 129, where we got to turn off one way or the other, I guess, but she shoots on across to another dirt road tucked in broomsage. I see lights coming up on the overpass. She cuts another circle, and brakes facing 129. A big truck goes *whoom!* Lights blowing up the hardroad before my eyes. Hit goes on. Hain't no point in saying, "Look out!" I just set there, cramping like I'm bear caught. She sets there too with her black-nailed hands on the steering wheel, like she's thinking. I guess she's scared cause we come in a wan of getting kilt, and now we'll head on to the house. Back behind us, in the east section of the quarters, the niggers is juking on a Saturday night. Loud sanging, hollering, younguns crying. Hain't nothing up against the racket of the car radio.

Directly, she reaches over and cuts the radio down and slings the fur wrop to the back seat, flapping me in my left eye with some button or something on the tail. I don't know what's coming up but I know we hain't fixing to go to the house.

"Give me your handkerchief," she says, turning her pink-cheeky face to me for the first time.

I feel like my hands is froze to the strop on the door.

"Give me your handkerchief," she says again, wagging her dirty right hand at me.

I dig hit out of my hip pocket, all streaked with blood and snot.

"You know how to break a dog from running cars?" she says.

"No, babe, can't say as I do." My eye stings, my nose is a spigot, blood running down my britches to the rat-fur gray seat.

She sees the blood, reaches back, and grabs the fur wrop, slinging hit to my lap; the tail snaps me in the eye again. Same eye. I taste blood from the inside now.

She gets out of the car and the inside lights up blurry bright. I hear her out messing around with the hubcap behind me, bury my nose in the fur, and watch her in the right-hand mirror, squatting down. She prizes off the hubcap, hammers hit back, and I see my handkerchief hanging out of the hubcap.

She gets back in and throws the car in gear, spins out

of the white sand and across 129. I got my right cheek pressed to the window glass, eyes fixed on the door mirror, watching my handkerchief spin on the hubcap like a loose whitewall tire. I hear the dog barking, then see hit dart up the dead-grass shoulder on my side, chasing after the wheel with the handkerchief. Red in the taillights with both front legs looking stuck together.

"Come on, you sonofabitch," says Sonia Lee. "I'm fixing to break you from running cars."

The dog lunges at the wheel, grabs holt of the handkerchief, and latches on, looping and wallowing in the spin of the wheel, then drops back to the ditch with one keen *yip*, flops, and lays broadside in the bleached grass.

Sonia Lee cackles out and steps on the gas, moving on up the road between the close-growing woods. "Broke his fucking neck," she says. I shet my eyes. She hain't my type. Her and Buster must be in cahoots. The good feeling I had before seems like a long time ago. Back before I was born. She turns the radio up again, and I don't try to make no sense out of the sanging. Over the river bridge again, out of Withers, before I get done thinking, If she stops this time, I'm gone get out and walk.

A couple of miles and she slows down and squalls off in another direction. South, I think. I don't open my eyes; hit won't make no difference anyhow, and I don't want to see the road in the dark ahead of the car lights running at me. I'm getting myself ready to die.

"You want to go back to my house?" she says.

I don't. I don't never want no more to do with some young heifer.

"Well, do you, huh?" she says.

I gotta answer. "Uh huh," I say, eyes shet tight, caught in a ball of cramps, my innards and all.

"What?" she hollers.

"Yep!" I holler back, figgering at least I might make hit back to Cornerville.

Lord, I say to the racing stars out the window, I got a few more things to do. Then I shet my eyes tight again.

"You like that song?" she says, turning up the radio.

"Yeah," I say and my one word don't go nowheres. I wish I could stop up my ears.

"You know what I wish, Old Man?"

"What?" I holler out.

"You know what I wish?" Louder.

"What?"

"I wish I could run over somebody."

I don't answer. I think hit's me, since they hain't nobody else around to run over. I open my eyes and look, trying to get my bearings, and the tall pines and scrub oaks and rusty fences is running away from us.

"I wish I could," she says. "I ain't killed nobody since I left Florida."

"Don't say!"

"Nope. I killed a man and woman once. You know how?"

"How come?"

"I don't know how come." She stalls talking a minute, like she's messed up, then goes on. "I kidnapped them, me and a old boy I was living with. Took 'em out in the woods and tied them to a tree. You know what we did next?"

"Nope."

"Shot 'em full of Drano."

"Drano?"

"You know, stuff you unclop sink pipes with."

She slows down to where the car hain't hardly moving, like she's out on a Sunday drive. I wish she'd speed up again. I like feeling cramped, I like feeling any way I can, long as I'm feeling. I keep my eyes shet.

"Know what else?" she says.

"Nope."

"What's that?"

"I say, what else?"

"I let 'em suffer awhile and then I cut 'em loose and stabbed 'em."

She's sanging right along with Elvis on the radio, and her voice sounds pitiful. But she hain't pitiful, she's mean. Done so much, she's got to go on to something harder to get her kicks. Like a dope fiend.

"See if they ain't something to drink in that glove box," she says, sanging, ". . . three to get ready, now go cat go. . . ."

I do like she says and look in the glove box. They's a flashlight, a map, and some papers with writing on them.

"Nope," I say, "just some papers and junk."

"What kind of papers?" she says.

I hand the folded sheets to her. She switches on a light inside, shakes out the papers, and reads them while she's driving.

I go back to my corner, like a turtle in a shell.

"Car-rent papers." She slaps the papers on the seat between us, flips off the overhead light. "Why, them old biddies!"

"Who?" I say.

"Your two sister-in-laws."

"Annie Bell and Rosanne?" I say. "This their car?"

"Yep," she says. I can hear how proud she is of herself. I don't want to see hit, go back to holding on to the strop and bracing myself, cause I got a good notion we fixing to lift off again.

We do. My neck presses back to the seat like hit's got me in a headlock. I can see the road behind my closed eyes; they might as well be open. My backend's made out of lead.

"Know what I'd like to do?" she says, slowing down.

"Oh, Lordy!" I whisper.

"Say?"

"Kill somebody?" I say.

"God, no!" she says like she even wouldn't think of hit. "I'd like to screw somebody royal."

"I hain't able," I say. "Look a-here, I'm old." I set up straight, feeble for real.

She laughs out, lights a cigarette, and I set watching her. I chunk the fur wrop in the back seat, hit wet with blood. My nose is stopped bleeding.

"I meant mess somebody up, their reputation," she says, gazing out the window.

I think about Buster. He hain't met his match. But I take pity on him, much as I despise him, and don't mention him.

"I could put some dope in this car and get your sister-in-laws sent off to the pen."

"Yeah," I say, then, "No."

"No!" she echoes. "What the hell you mean, 'No?'" Her face is white and blowed up in the dashlights. Her brown eyes look wild. But she looks like a little girl just learning to drive.

We get to another crossroad and she turns left and I see a sign says 94. A word beside the numbers, but I can't read hit. East, maybe hit's east, maybe we heading back toward Cornerville. I get my bearings now: Sonia Lee has made the square up 129 to Withers, west to the next fork, then south to 94, now east. Seems like we been halfway round the world, and all we done is squared off a section of Swanoochee County.

Sometimes she drives on the left side of the hardroad, sometimes on the right, but we don't meet nobody. Nothing but woods. I'm glad I'm heading home, but I hain't there yet.

She stops in the middle of the hardroad and punches in the car lighter and waits, watching me. When the lighter clicks, she yanks hit out and holds the red coils to the tip of my nose where I can just feel the heat. I don't move. Then she stretches out a long piece of her hair and sticks the lighter to the end, watching hit singe and curl. She lets hit burn out, her eyes as dead as the glass eyes of a blind man.

I hain't never thought I'd say hit, but I wish the law would come up on us.

She shoots the car ahead again, and I get sucked back in the seat. I close my eyes and inch over to my corner, getting as used to hit as my chair at home. From behind my eyelids, I spy the red light blinking at the Cornerville crossing. The car slows down and I sneak a peep at the red light, still a ways off. We're on the Alapaha bridge at the Cornerville city-limits sign, and I bet we've beat the river water running from the bridge in Withers to here.

"I think I'll jump in the river," she says, eyeing me.

"Would you take this car home first?" I say. "I can't drive."

"You're too old for me, Old Man," she says.

"I know hit."

Pee Wee

All of a sudden, I ain't drunk no more. I'm stomach-rolling sober. Like I'm a sailor again and we're moving out to another port, and being drunk's a luxury you can't afford. Sober up or you'll wish you had of, and you can do it, since coming up's another port where you can get drunk and forget the sober time behind you and the one coming up, and that's how you make it, civilian or sailor, every day, and sometimes they run together, drunk and sober, to a blur. That's what you shoot for, your goal.

I'm traveling light now, like I do, sober. They're all back there in the truck, Earl, Alamand, Buck, and a bunch more old hard-tail boys. And I'm by myself, looking out for number one. I don't know how number one got into this, but if it don't go to suit me when I get there, I'm gone.

I can feel the situation rising like puke in my throat, and I'm used to the taste of it.

Backing out of the woods, the truck's in my control, like I'm driving, standing here on the edge, acting like I'm raring to go. I know what I'm raring to go to, too. Bootlegging. I been there before and it ain't all that different from nothing else, just a dry time, skin-crawling stiff. Buck's always running his last load of shine. But I know another time will come up, and we'll be running shine again. Hear me! Not he, but we. Buck ain't never done nothing by hisself; gotta get me into it. I oughta be kicked for coming home from the service. Home! Sounds good when you're off; it ain't. Ends don't meet when you get there, and then to make them meet, to get enough money, you gotta run another load of shine. Somebody else will lay down and die or something. That's what life is: death.

Poor old Mama. Everybody's so busy trying to get her buried, ain't nobody had the time or sense to make over her. Maybe none of us can't since she's better off dead, and seeing her every day, toting firewood and water, trying to come up with another meal, putting up with us and the old man, is worse. Suffering. That's how I see her face, and the word "mama" won't never mean nothing but suffering to me. Laboring and labor pains.

You don't see that in Sonia Lee. When Sonia Lee dies, she'll just set back and quit breathing, no better off, no worse off. Just another whore dead that don't bring to mind suffering. She's like a empty conch shell that won't rot since nothing ain't never been inside her.

The night is thick cold, and in around the diesel fumes from the truck I can smell my own puke. That's part of sobering up. I ain't cold; I can't afford it. I ain't sick neither, and I ain't scared. Just setting ready in case things go sour. More than likely, we'll head out and unload at another woods road and pick up a car loaded with shine and run it on over to Jennings, Florida, or some other little hick town where the law needs a little get-by money bad as we do. You can't never tell. That's Boss Purvis I seen driving, and he likes to bully a bunch of boys to keep them in line. Then we're supposed to belong to him and Buster and the other big shots till we lay down and die. I'd just as soon haul shine as fence posts, for sixty cents apiece, or put up shit houses. But I ain't taking no crap. It's every man for hisself.

Last time I placed some dependence on Buck, he come in a wan of getting us both killed. Soon as we got in that old souped-up Chevy, he mashed down on the gas and didn't let up till we'd busted through two roadblocks. The first one, nobody wadn't even looking for shine, they was checking drivers' licenses. Buck rammed two sheriff cars that night, me setting on the other side, scared shitless, and then he outrun the law in two counties by cutting down woods roads, doing ninety-to-nothing. We finally hopped out and left the car running, high-tailing it through the woods back to Cornerville. When I asked Buck how come him run through that first roadblock, he just drawed up in a knot and said, "I can't help it. When I see the law, I just run."

The truck backs out slow to the highway and then straightens up and heads south down the long lonesome stretch to Jennings. They ain't nothing but a loud vibration from where I'm standing, cold air shooting all around me, but I can smell the fear coming off Buck and them boys back there like musk off a snake. You can end up taking the rap for the big boys, or the big boys can shoot you dead and make it look like you done it to one another. Could be setting right there on the jury, the big boys could, if you're caught and tried. That's how you get hooked. Either way you're a loser. But the money always sounds good rattling in the big shots' pockets.

I grin to myself since I know, since I can't be got to.

The sky looks like the inside of a leaky tent in the middle of the day, sharp stars for holes. The night's swole up, a steel gray, like it might bust wide open from the least motion.

We go on past the road where I figgered we'd turn off, so I grip the rope I'm hanging to tighter, feeling my skin crawl.

Loujean

_____ **O**ut front, I hear a car pulling up or leaving one; the baby's crying so loud I can't tell which. Getting to where I'm hearing things, I guess, but it's about time for the transfer trucks passing through Cornerville to be pulling up and parking for the night.

I strip the baby and put her on another outing gown the county nurse brung me. I don't know how many clean diapers I've got left, but I know I need to put out a washing. I feel better working anyhow. Since I told everybody Mama's corpse ain't coming home, I ain't got to put on airs no more. Up to now, I been acting like my aunts must of acted at my age.

I let my breath go and pick up the baby, holding her close. She's still crying.

"Colic," Miss Amaretta says, standing over me. "You got any paregoric, sweetie?"

"No um, I don't think so."

"I'll run go get some from the house then."

"What in the world?" I hear Aunt Rosanne say. I don't want to know; she's probably just found out her fur stole's missing. I see her leant over the old man's chair, looking out the front window. Her head's hid behind the curtain and her broad fanny's sticking out. "You parked right at the door, didn't you, sister?" she calls back to Aunt Annie Bell on the couch.

For all their "making something out of theirselfs," as they say, they still talk just like us late at night when they're wore out. And too, I guess, they don't think we're worth playacting for no more. The right person could come through that door, and who knows how they'd talk.

"I did," says Aunt Annie Bell. "Parked it right out front."

Aunt Rosanne stands there a minute with her head still behind the curtain, and Aunt Annie Bell wallows up from the couch and pads in her stocking feet across the room to the front window. They act like nobody else ain't here but them. In their minds, they ain't. I done heared Aunt Rosanne telling about the "quaint" lil ole house in Tarver where they was born and raised by good God-fearing "parents." The house was a rundown shack, their daddy was mean as a snake, their mama drunk herself to death. Everybody around here knows that story. So, in the last few hours, Aunt Annie Bell looks like she's caught on—the cat's out of the bag—and is nearly bout her true self.

"That is not my car," says Aunt Annie Bell, peeping out the window with Aunt Rosanne. "Looks like the hearse bringing Louella."

Her revived proper tone takes a front-row seat to what she's just said, at first, then my heart lifts. I don't care who's done what, how they sound, long as it's true. I wait for somebody to say that it is Aunt Annie Bell's car after all. I hang back, patting the baby on my shoulder, and watch everybody shove out the door. Not nearly bout as many people going out as it looked like and them crowded in the room.

Miss Amaretta, ahead of me, says, "Praise the Lord!" and gazes up at the ceiling.

I wish I'd of thought to sweep the cobwebs down, I think as I go to the door. But then when I see the long black hearse parked on the cement slope, people all around, laughing and talking, I don't care. Should we be rejoicing, like the Bible says, or crying? I don't know, but I laugh out loud with the baby bawling in my ear.

"Joyful Noise," I whisper in her face—beautiful, raw, and bawling.

From the café to the courtyard to the cement slope between the house and the highway, transfer trucks are lining up, parking and idling down for the night.

The transfers' snoring, mixed with the baby's crying and the mourners' laughing, is like nothing I ever heard before. A party. Two men in black suits open the back doors of the hearse, and between the wine velvet curtains on the windows, I see a bronze casket sliding out, bright as fire in the lights of the transfers behind it. A blanket of yellow roses trembles on top like Mama's spirit is seeping up from the casket.

When they get the casket set up on a rolling stand with a wine skirt, they wheel it up the slope to the board-walk, lift up, and set it inside the door, and I step back and watch it shine in the drab room. My eyes tear up, but I'm still laughing. Aunt Rosanne and Aunt Annie Bell follow it inside with the others on their heels. Aunt Annie Bell goes around Aunt Rosanne and stands before the couch. "Place it right over here," she says to the men. Then to the people behind them, "Be a sweetheart, ladies and gentlemen, and pull this couch out from the wall. Please."

"If you put it there, it'll get the heat from the stove," says Miss Amaretta, crossing to the plant shelf in the corner. "Put it over here. We'll just move these plants out to the kitchen if you fellows will wait a minute."

"Over here," says Aunt Annie Bell, ignoring Miss Amaretta and watching the couch glide to the middle of the room ahead of Uncle Albert.

Sultana, mother-in-law tongue, hen and biddies, begonias, wandering Jew—all pass before me in a trail of ladies. The men with the casket are already pushing it toward the dusty rectangle where the couch used to be.

"Right over here," says Miss Amaretta, standing in place of the plant stand. A dirty comb and a cigarette pack glare at me.

The men slide the casket from the middle of the wall, past the mantelshelf, to the corner.

"Is the woman in the coffin your sister?" Aunt Annie Bell asks Miss Amaretta and steps to the spot where the couch has shed its dust. "I didn't think so," she answers, motioning for the men with the casket like she's directing traffic.

The casket rolls on squealing wheels back toward the strange empty space under the busted side window, home of the couch.

"It's too hot over there," says Miss Amaretta.

The casket stops under the mantelshelf, the men wait.

Aunt Annie Bell trots over to Miss Amaretta with her hands on her girdled hips. "That fire business is so old-fashioned!" she says. "Besides, who's paying for all this?"

I wonder too. I know we're s'posed to think my aunts are paying, but I doubt it. They're as surprised and excited as everybody else, just have a little more practice at acting cool.

"Y'all can leave it right there," I say to the men. They step away and stand, watching us.

Aunt Annie Bell steps behind the casket and pushes it to the spot where the couch was, toes turned up in her black stockings.

"Now," she says, brushing her hands, "we'll put the flowers in the corner."

Uncle Albert lugs the shelf stand back to the corner, and the ladies holding the plants parade back to the shelf.

"Not them!" Aunt Annie Bell shrieks. "The florist's stock. *Nck nck nck!*"

The men in black suits ease out the door, and in a few minutes, two men in white uniforms come in with sprays of glads and carnations, placing them on stands in the corner. They go out and come back in with more flowers, and again they go out and come back in. More flowers.

I pick up the comb and cigarette pack in the growing garden of flowers, ashamed of smiling and showing my feelings. I can't believe it—flowers! Styrofoam crosses, hearts, and wreaths covered in roses and lilies and ferns. "Ma'am," calls one of the men through the door to anybody who might be in charge, "you want the rest of the flowers left out here on the porch? There's lots more." He holds up a wreath of purple and pink flowers the size of a tractor tire.

"That large wreath will do fine in here," says Aunt Annie Bell, prancing to the door. "The others can stay outside. Be fresher for tomorrow."

More! I want to see them, I want Mama to see them. I want to see Mama. I look at the baby, so limp she's like a shoulder pad now, and hand her to Miss Amaretta and go out the door.

The boardwalk, running in a ell around the side and back of the house, is banked with flowers of every kind and color. The cold piney air starts smelling like a funeral. I'm not even cold anymore, but my teeth are chattering. I spy a white van on the other side of the hearse and watch as the two men in white pluck more flowers from the back and set them on the cement slope. So rich and strange and bright against the oil puddles on the sidewalk, against the burnt-diesel smell of the transfer trucks. I wish Mama could see them there since she never had a front yard to plant flowers in, just the pots inside with cuttings the neighbors give her.

Still in her stocking feet, Aunt Annie Bell trots along the boardwalk, rearranging the flowers as the men set them up on the boardwalk. She must be freezing to death, but her face just looks fixed for business.

"If you've got any more," she calls to the men, "bring them back tomorrow for the funeral." She pads quick from the corner of the boardwalk to the front, blowing into her hands, then tips out and down the cement slope to the hearse. "What time has the undertaker got down for the funeral tomorrow?" she whispers to one of the men.

"Three o'clock," he says.

"Where?"

"At the Church of Sinners in Cornerville."

"Correct," she says and scoots back up the slope to the boardwalk, hugging herself. "Be a little early for the procession. Please," she calls back. And then to herself, "Church of Sinners?"

Inside, she closes the door and grabs her fur stole off the back of the couch in the middle of the room, and wraps it around her shoulders and heads for the stove to warm.

"Move that couch to the foot of the bed there," she says to Uncle Albert, standing hunched, humble, and ready. "And somebody be a sweetheart and get me a cup of hot coffee. Some cake would be lovely too."

I want to catch her before she gets full and cross again. Aunt Rosanne's already working on a piece of German chocolate cake, and everybody else is talking and wandering. Some of them's reading the cards on the flowers.

"My name's on this one!" says Miss Tissie, like she just won a prize. "Who in the world?"

Yes, I think, who? Was it the tooth fairy, Mama? You said they wadn't no tooth fairy the time you got tired of lying and saying he couldn't find my tooth under my pillow was how come he didn't leave me no money. There is a tooth fairy, Mama.

"Can I open up the casket?" I ask Aunt Annie Bell, now perched on the couch at the foot of the bed. A forkful of coconut cake lifts from her shaking hand to her pink open mouth. "Just a minute, child," she says. She bites into the cake, swallows, pats her chest, dabs at her lips with the corner of a paper towel, then sips her coffee. The diamond heart on her stuffed neck quivers. She coughs into her fist.

"Let's not," she finally says. "Opening the coffin would be too morbid." She forks more cake to her greedy mouth.

"Would it be too morbid," I say, "if I slip the coffin down under the mantelshelf to get a piece of firewood?"

I don't wait for her to answer; I go over and shove the warm end of the bronze casket till the other end is flush with the flowers in the corner. While arranging the flowers, Mama's houseplants included, little by little, Miss Amaretta inches the casket along the wall till it's where she wanted it in the first place.

As I reach through the window to get a piece of wood, somebody sweeps under my feet. Bad luck: I might never get married now. I let the window down again, and in the paint-black glass I picture Earl's face like it was through the window this evening when he brought the load of oak. I'd like to marry him someday, I would. I got all idears he's the tooth fairy had Mama brung home. But how?

"Thank you," I say to the window.

Putting the wood in the stove, I make up my mind it'll be the last piece burnt till Mama's gone, old-fashioned or not. I poke up the fire and close the stove door, and when I look back at the casket, I see Miss Amaretta's got the lid raised and is straightening a wine veil over Mama's face. Aunt Undine's cradling the blanket of yellow roses in her arms. The rest of the old man's kin passes by the casket, heartpine faces gazing down at Mama.

I look over at Aunt Annie Bell, on her second slice of cake now, then go over to the casket.

Mama's got on a sweet pink church dress with a Peter Pan collar and pearls that hook from point to point of the collar. White gloves hide her chapped hands. Her gray hair is waved like she just come back from the beauty parlor, and her face is made up with some flat ivory makeup and pink rouge. She's smiling sad, like she'd do on the verge of crying. I lift the veil and kiss her cool waxy face.

"I named the baby Joyful Noise," I whisper.

My shadow on her face makes the liver pieds on her forehead show through the makeup. I fix the veil back. I don't even feel like crying, but a bunch of the women is sobbing in their handkerchiefs.

"She looks just like herself," one says.

"Like she could set up and go to talking," says another one.

Aunt Rosanne, done eating and seeing the lid raised, comes over and bellers for ten minutes right over Mama. It's the most honest thing I've seen her do. I feel sorrier for her than I ever have for Mama.

Aunt Annie Bell sets there on the couch, pressing crumbs with her fork. In a minute, she calls for somebody to be a sweetheart and come get her plate, then rolls her arms in her fur stole and rares back. This time she sleeps, snoring like the trucks outside. I know she's relieved. We have that much in common. Shuddering peacefully, Aunt Rosanne finally goes and sets down in the old man's chair. I think about going over and hugging her, but decide she's the kind to grieve by herself.

I go to the bed and set in the middle with my legs curled under me to warm. Eyes on the casket. I hear somebody go out the front door, then another. Miss Amaretta comes to the bed and tells me they's a bunch of them going home to sleep for a spell, then coming back to relieve the ones staying. I nod.

The room needed thinning out. The roses smell like rat bait, much as I love them. I set in the same spot, purring like a cat on the inside, till I hear Aunt Rosanne sliding the old man's chair across the floor, searching for something.

Buck

They must be a dozen of us old boys huddled close to the cab on back of the truck, hassling like dogs. I can't see nobody but Pee Wee, solid cocked in the open frame of cold gray before me. Big truck makes us feel littler, like we don't matter. I guess hauling us like a load of shoats is part of how Buster and them aims to get our attention. You gotta hand it to him, he's a genius when it comes to thinking up ways to scare the hell out of a bunch of boys.

I got a feeling some of these boys is here for the first time, getting broke into the club. Ain't my first time, but being as how I cut loose the last time, I'm looking for a lesson from Buster, who you can bet ain't along for the ride. Like I said, he don't run a danger of getting caught with the goods. It'd be right helpful to know what he told the driver, though, so we could be on the lookout.

Hunkering beside me, Earl feels stiff. Out of all of us here, he's the most serious now, and I swear and be damned if I don't wish he'd lighten up. If he would, I know somehow we'd come out on top. You can depend on Earl, normally, to turn things around just by cutting the fool. I don't know if he cuts up like he does out of ignorance, or if he knows that taking life too serious will make you draw up and die. The floorboards of the truck is study beating us, like pounding steak for frying. I figger these boys, specially Alamand, blowing on my neck, is scareder than I am, and that's gotta be one hell. Cause I'm scared. I done been down this road before, me and Pee Wee. He might look like a soldier, but I know in a jam he won't be no help. Everlast one of these boys is mine since I'm likely the oldest, since I'm the one's been there.

The truck's gearing down. Pee Wee's peeping out around the side.

"Earl," I say in his ear, "when we stop, you stay here with Alamand and let the rest of us unload. Wait till we get gone good, then y'all light out through the woods. You hear?"

"What's that, Buck?" he breathes back.

The truck stops moving, the engine quits roaring. I smell willow trees and water, hear frogs blatting. I whisper it to him again, and I can feel him gazing in my face. "I'm here to work," he says and scrambles up, wobbling out toward the back of the truck with a line of boys behind.

The cab of the truck springs, a door slams, the hood squawks.

I turn to tell Alamand to stay put, ain't nobody expecting him, but then I see him stumbling out behind Earl, his dark stocky body gray-framed, shuffling foot to foot and bouncing to the ground. "All right, you nincompoops!" yells a man from the front of the truck. "Step there against the body of the truck and don't wet on yourselfs." He laughs out, just as I come up on the tail end of the line and step back with them. We're on a wood bridge with water guggling under it. Must be Little River, just out of Jennings. Middle of nowhere. Nothing but a scratchy sound coming from the truck hood, the shrieking of katydids, and frogs bloating the dark with bellowing. A pulse of in-held breaths from the truck body to the cab. No light, save for the stars over and beyond the bridge rail where cypress trees poke through the bristle-smear of pines. And looking down, as far as you can see in the starshine, water like melted iron.

And then light. A strong beam shooting from the front of the truck, out over the river and woods, then down the alley of wide boards with cracks of lit, riffling water between the line of boys and the wood railing. Behind the beam, toting what looks like a thirty-thirty rifle in one hand and a airplane light in the other, is Boss Purvis, one of the big shots I done had some dealings with. Red meaty face and jowls, great gut and stumpy legs, khaki pants riding low on his narrow hips. A black cord trails from the light to the truck hood and slides over two cement blocks, front and center of the railing we stand facing. Heading my way, the light flies from face to face, while Boss cusses one and then the other. Now and then calling somebody by name—Jackknife and Rabbit, nicknames I know have to do with past dealings with him— but passing right over Alamand, four boys down from me, like Alamand's just juice in the soup.

I let my breath go. Light moving toward me, landing on the face of the tall, skinny boy on my right—black-headed with pimples, set blue eyes. "Bo Peep," snorts Boss.

"Purvis," says Bo Peep—whatever the hell that means. The light slams me, I see firecracker sparkles in it.

"Well, well, well," says Boss, backing to get a better look, satisfied, "if it ain't Scurvy."

No nickname, no favors. I'm it, I figger.

Boss backs to the bridge rail, leans and props a giant foot on one of the cement blocks.

I hear Alamand shuffling his feet on the wood bridge. I want to tell him to stay still. He's bad to pace when he gets nervous.

"Boys, I stopped here on purpose," Boss says, walking with the light again, end to end of the boys lined along the truck. "Any of y'all got a idear what it is?"

Alamand grunts. I wait for the light to slam him, but Boss is talking, walking, bullying somebody at the other end. Maybe Pee Wee, who I'd of thought would of been long gone by now.

"Well," Boss says, "I tell you how it is." He steps to the bridge rail and shines the light on the boiling black water, closer to the bridge than it looked in the dark, then parades with the light before us again. "A few of y'all—I ain't gone call no names," he says—the light slams me and he picks up talking where he left off—"is been knowed to run out on a job. You don't do that, boys. This ain't no tea party."

He's standing right in front of me now, bowed up like a rooster fixing to crow. "Do you, Buck?"

"No sir," I say, hot as fire. The rest of the boys is got the truck a-rocking they so cold and scared. I'm hemmed up by the light, fixing to be made a example of. Last time I run a load, I just quit; didn't never show up again. I sent what money I could to Buster, give it to Miss Cleta at the post office to pass on to him. Buster and them don't keep close records and ain't too concerned about where a man's paid up or not.

The light leaps from my face to the boiling black water just under the bridge. Boss follows it. "Come over here, boys," he says. "I want to show y'all something pretty." Buster couldn't of picked no better teacher to put the fear of God in us.

We all step up together, like we're chained by the ankles, looking over the bridge rail like school younguns on a outing.

"Look down there, boys," says Boss, shining the light from bank to bank: willows and tupelos bogged and wringing in the current. A gray-pied moccasin braided on a snag. A log floats by, sucks under in a whorl and shoots up. He spotlights it, flowing downriver in sudden fog.

I'm watching the show, but thinking about the black cord trailing from the light to the truck hood, where it must hook to the battery. If I could get to the other side of Boss, I could yank it loose and cut the light. Then we could overtake him before he gets down to business; this is just the buildup before the boom. But it's subject to be just me and old tub-of-guts tussling, cause these boys is done cowed. And Boss Purvis is liable to have a hired gun close by as a backup. But best I remember, he prides hisself on not needing nobody else. I cut my eyes to the right, trying to pick out his backup from the row of scared-stiff boys, all gazing down, but I can't see behind without turning my head, and I know Boss's eyes ain't on nobody else but me.

"Little River, out of banks. Ain't that a pretty sight,

boys?" Boss says, looking at me. All of us together could chunk him over the bridge. But I guess these boys knows they'd have to run for the rest of their lives. Home's too precious, somebody's waiting on us, needing us.

Out of the blue, Boss swings the light around, turns tough. "Now, y'all get your asses back over yonder like you was."

The boys scamper to the truck, pressing their backs to the body.

Boss walks with the light toward me. "They's one or two of y'all don't take us serious, I can tell."

Me and Pee Wee, I think.

"So, like they do in school, boys, I'm gone learn y'all a lesson."

My face goes to burning. I hope Pee Wee's gone.

"And the best way I can think of to learn y'all a lesson is by example. Want to show you where you might end up if you so much as think about cutting out on us."

I feel crazy, couldn't run now if I tried, go to thinking how the old man, even sorry as he is, is subject to get real sentimental if me and Pee Wee both dies trying to get the money to put Mama away cause he, the old man, couldn't take on another funeral after going all out on Aunt Becky's, buying that extra-long casket to keep the undertaker from breaking her upraised, locked arms, like Buster suggested. The old man might have to go to Buster for mine and Pee Wee's funeral money, then die his ownself and leave Loujean whoring right there back of Buster's old store to pay Buster back the money. I get a good look at Boss, almost at me now: blood veins on his bloated neck, flush with his face, bogged blue eyes, hawk nose. The light shoots to my face, sucks me in like a waterwhorl. "Now," he says, "who's gone volunteer for a example?"

Nobody don't move. I can't. The light's like a steel cage around me. My heart feels like somebody's running a stick along my ribs. Blind, I hear the frogs and katydids shriller. A owl yowls over the river.

"What I need's somebody to step right up here and let me tie this cement block to his foot and bail in."

The light goes wild, up and down the line, then stops on the cement blocks next to Boss's right foot. I know one of them's got my initials on it. The light flips to the other end of the line, and I figger Pee Wee ain't split after all, and the other block's got his initials on it. But I think to myself that Boss is about got other plans for tonight, other lessons coming up tonight, that this is just a warm-up exercise and all we got to do is act interested and scared shitless. Which ain't all that hard to do.

"Do I have a volunteer?" Boss hollers.

He sets the light on the railing so it's shining up the highway through the tunnel of trees, then lifts the rifle and breaches it—*schlp!* The sound echoes out over the river and woods and strikes on the bridge like a match. Holding the stock to his right shoulder, he levels the barrel over the line of boys till he gets to me.

"Do I have a volunteer?" he repeats, this time low and final.

"Last one in's a rotten egg!" Earl hollers from the other end of the line.

Quicker than light, he shoots from the line to the railing and dives—*streak, thump, plash*—and looks like the rest of the boys on his end is tethered to him. *Streak, thump, plash*—over the railing they go, lifting the line of boys from the other end of the truck body all the way to me. Boss, cussing, turning, whirling, knocks the light to the bridge floor and spins it with his boot as he swings the rifle over the railing and back, searching for me, I guess, among the dodging, diving bodies. I go for it, up and over and down to the iron water, darkness, and roaring silence, like a sudden sweep of memories.

Loujean

Sprawled out on the couch, Aunt Annie Bell's got the crown of her head aimed at me on the bed. Her varnished blond curls are mashed flat on the back and sides from where she's been wallowing. Ever so often, she wakes herself up with her own snoring. She shifts, snuggles into her mink stole, sleeps.

Aunt Rosanne is mumbling to herself, looking behind the old man's chair.

I feel like I'm watching a picture show. I don't care about her mink stole that's been stole. I just watch Mama and keep praying: Thank you, Lord; thank you, Earl. I can't wait to see him again, keep thinking about what he said the morning after Mama died: Looks like old Loujean there's just setting taking it easy. I should of knowed he'd come up with something. He ain't dumb as he looks.

Aunt Rosanne, searching for her fur, is really going hog-wild now, but everybody else is still and peaceful, like after a fight. All sleepy, cold, waiting for daybreak. Setting in the chairs along the walls, the ladies look like they're nodding, but I figger they're watching Aunt Rosanne too.

More ladies is out in the kitchen, washing dishes and cramming food in the Frigidaire. A muffled dim night clatter to let you know they're in charge, that they're there in case you want tea or food or talk. Aunt Rosanne goes over to the casket, gets down on her hands and knees, and peeps under the wine velvet skirt. "What in the world could've come of it?" she mumbles.

I wonder how long it'll take her to recollect Sonia Lee standing behind the old man's chair, looking neither guilty or not-guilty before she swiped the mink. I wonder how many of these ladies, setting up with Mama, has come up missing a pot or pan, a ring maybe. The ring Sonia Lee stole from me come out of a bubble-gum machine, and she had the gall to wear it right in front of me. Like she done it for meanness and was daring me to take it back.

Aunt Rosanne walks back to the old man's chair and sets down with her hands folded under her chin, like she's praying to the Lord for a answer to what could of come of her stole. In a minute, she starts gazing at the mourners along the wall—all eyes closed now. I close mine too, leaving a peep space between the lids. She scoots to the edge of the chair with her legs spread, black dress stretched across her stout knees, then stands and tiptoes across the room, gazing back at Mama. The floorboards squeak under her feet and she stops, checks everybody out again, then creeps on over to the couch where Aunt Annie Bell's snoring with her feet stuck out and her bunioned toes stuck up.

Aunt Rosanne steps around Aunt Annie Bell's feet and places a hand on the mink stole like she's checking for a blood pulse. She tugs at it. Aunt Annie Bell snorts and rolls her arms in the fur, and Aunt Rosanne lets go, waiting till she's snoring regular again, then tugs at it again. Aunt Annie Bell rolls her head to one side, smacks her lips. Mashed-down curls make her face look sharp. The fire's died down in the heater and cold air's seeping through the wall at my back that separates Buster's old store from our house. I need to put another blanket over the baby in her drawer by the bed. But not yet; I'm dying to see what my aunts will do.

Mama looks like she's waiting too.

Miss Amaretta, setting by the casket, peeps and smiles, then snuggles into her black overcoat.

Aunt Rosanne reaches for Aunt Annie Bell's fur stole again, watching her like a snake, and drags it down her stuffed-stockinged legs. She snorts, but goes on snoring. Aunt Rosanne backs up, still dragging the stole, and gets halfway across the room before Aunt Annie Bell starts rolling her arms in the air.

She sets up and stares at Aunt Rosanne dragging her fur stole like a youngun dragging a blanket. "What do you think you're doing?" says Aunt Annie Bell, fluffing her curls till they stick out like broomstraw.

"Taking back my mink stole, that's what."

Aunt Annie Bell leaps up, jarring the bowls and platters on the eating table, and still the others in the room either sleep or make like they're sleeping.

I really need to cover the baby now. I peep down at her in the drawer and she's sucking her thumb. I wonder who she looks like and if it's true that if you're a pretty baby you'll be ugly when you grow up.

Aunt Annie Bell walks over to Aunt Rosanne, bends

down, and yanks the tail of the fur on the floor. Aunt Rosanne hangs tight to the other end. "Don't you dare rip it," says Aunt Annie Bell. "Turn loose."

"It's mine," says Aunt Rosanne, backing and towing Aunt Annie Bell about a foot.

"It ain't yours, it's mine," Aunt Annie Bell says. "Yours ain't real, this one is."

"Mine is real!" Aunt Rosanne backs toward the old man's chair like it's home base. "Yours ain't."

Aunt Annie Bell now has hold of the stole halfway up the middle. "Look at this," she says, holding up a label on the inside. "GENUINE MINK, it says."

"A genuine mink doesn't have to say it's genuine," says Aunt Rosanne, letting go. "I got mine from Lord & Taylor."

"Lord & Taylor my hind leg!" Aunt Annie Bell slings the stole about her shoulders and holds it in place. "You probably left yours in the car."

The car. The car is gone. My eyes fly wide, like the picture playing out on the back of my eyelids will go away if I don't look. I remember now, remember going out when the hearse come and seeing the transfer trucks, the white flower van, and the black shiny hearse in place of Aunt Annie Bell's black shiny car. I look over at Miss Amaretta and figger she's remembering too, because she's setting up straight, gazing at the front door like she can see through it.

Aunt Rosanne sets down in the old man's chair, pouting and shaking in the cold air coming around the seam of the door.

Aunt Annie Bell sets down on the couch and rolls her arms in the fur again. She rares back, grits her teeth, and says, "Go out there and get your Lord & Taylor mink, but you better not mess with mine." Here we go!

Aunt Rosanne just sets there rocking, shivering, nodding. Looks like she's going to sleep. I'm afraid now to get up and cover the baby cause I might set her off. I get up anyway, take a blanket off the bed and spread it over the baby, drawer and all, leaving the head uncovered, and tuck the sides down around her. I hear Aunt Rosanne shifting in the chair, and I look to see if she's getting up to go to the car that's not there. She gets still again, rubbing her arms to get the blood circulating, I guess. Maybe if I can get her warm, she'll drop off to sleep. I take my quilt Mama made me with the red and blue stars from the foot of the bed and take it to her.

"Here, Aunt Rosanne," I say, holding out the quilt.

She takes it, sniffs it, feels it. "Peed on," she says and drops it to the floor. "I'll just go get my fur."

"Let me," I say.

She grunts.

I feel like letting her go, letting her go and find the car gone. Let her call up the law and have Sonia Lee and the old man put in jail.

I open the door and the cold air's like all the other walls I keep walking into.

Going out the door, I smell the flowers, sweet in the burnt-diesel reek of simmering truck engines. From the door to the corner of the boardwalk, they look froze and colorless, but under the front window, where the light from inside shines through the curtains, they look like flowers blooming in the sun. On the cement slope, where the hearse was

setting, is just a oily patch, and behind it the line of transfers idling from Buster's old store south to the café. A film
of white smoke dims the blinking red light at the crossing.
Could be Aunt Annie Bell's car is parked between the
transfer closest to me and the one behind it, I think, and
head out to check. At the first truck, I look up high
through the gray-tinted window and see the driver sleeping with his head back on the seat. One of them strangers
Mama used to tell me to look out for, same as she'd tell me
to look out for mad dogs. I never did listen, never did
think of the truck drivers as strangers—not really. Didn't
seem half as strange as my own family. I wonder what
would happen if I was to knock on this tall, dusty blue
truck door and go to talking to the driver. Would he
understand if I told him my mama died from uremic poisoning after having a baby and left it with me and it cries
three-fourths of the time, and for a while there it looked
like Mama wadn't gone get buried because the undertaker
wouldn't take her till we paid off the debt for Aunt Becky's
funeral, which the old man went all out for to keep the
undertaker from breaking her arms where they'd locked
overhead from holding Alamand up to keep him from
drownding in the well? What if I told him about Buster
and Great-Uncle John and the ongoing feud over him
leaving his money to the county, and how I finally get
Mama home because of this boy named Earl in a yellow
shirt and now looks like I ain't gone be able to round
everybody up for her funeral tomorrow? He wouldn't
understand.

When I get to the next truck, idling this side of the
crossing, I see the car ain't parked between the two trucks,

that it's for real gone now, the old man's gone, Sonia Lee's gone. And looking up at the next driver through the window of his red truck, sleeping with his head on the steering wheel, I wonder what he'd say if I said, I'm out looking for this car belongs to one of my aunts, which my own daddy and his girlfriend stole after sneaking out at my mama's wake with a mink stole belonging to my other aunt. How could I say all that and make him understand without going into everything else? No stranger, without knowing our background, couldn't piece it all together.

I go on back and set down on the boardwalk, hugging myself against the cold.

What if the old man and Sonia Lee don't come back? What will I tell my aunts? Why does everything have to get spoiled? Now the old man might go to jail and us with a funeral coming up. He's been there before, guilty or not, when Buster got bored or the old man got in the way. And so it goes, round and round, and if I can't piece it all together, how in the world could some stranger piece it all together? I look at the truck closest to me again, through the windshield at the sleeping driver, and think how I've always thought of these trucks as the same trucks, the same drivers, every night since I can remember, and suddenly I know they're not the same and that seems important, wakes me up. Every night a new stranger sleeps out front of our house. Every night! They are strangers and strangers can't never know us, can't know this place here and what-all happens day to day, what holds us together. And I know it's the same for the truck drivers, just a different picture on a jigsaw puzzle.

Old Man

When Sonia Lee takes a left at the crossing, I figger she's gone get me right up to the house, then take off about the time I go to bail out.

"You're too old for me," she says again and pulls in ahead of the lead transfer on the cement slope.

I see Loujean setting on the boardwalk and start to get out, since I know hit hain't gone be that easy to part ways with Sonia Lee.

Loujean sees us, gets up, and steps to the front of the hot idling car, and I don't know what to do. If I get out now, Sonia Lee's subject to run over her; if I set here, she's subject to drive off with me in the car. I stay. If she tries anything I'll stop her.

Loujean props on the car hood, eyeballing Sonia Lee through the windshield. "You better hand over that mink stole, you thief," Loujean says. She grits her teeth; her freckledy face blinks red, then white, in the blinking red light at the crossing.

Sonia Lee just sets, foot on the gas, one hand playing with her hair and the other playing with the gear shift. I'm getting set to snatch her hand if she yanks down. "And if I don't give it back?" she calls out the window.

"If you don't, I'll see to it you go to the pen." Loujean puts her hands on her hips and spraddles her legs, like she'll block the car if hit starts moving.

"Says who?" Sonia Lee mashes the gas, the engine winds up, winds down.

"Says Aunt Annie Bell, and she's with the GBI in Etlanna. That good enough for you?"

Sonia Lee reaches back and grabs the fur wrop. I duck. She slings hit out the window. Loujean lunges around the car, misses the wrop, picks hit up, and shakes out the fur like a live fox. "Now," she says to Sonia Lee, "I'll take the car keys too."

Sonia Lee smiles, mashes the gas, but takes her hand off the gear shift. She switches off the car, snatches the ring of keys free, leans out the window, and drops them to the cement. Loujean bends down to pick them up. Sonia Lee props both arms in the window, hanging out and laughing. The car ticks like a clock. The idling transfers pick up humming where the car engine left off.

"Now, get on home," says Loujean, yanking open the door before Sonia Lee can draw back inside. She tumbles out to the cement slope.

I figger she's fixing to grab Loujean now, but she gets up and stumbles off up the hardroad, then down the Troublesome Creek dip.

"Get on in the house, old man," Loujean says. "Mama's home."

I get out and try to hide how glad I am. I didn't expect hit; I don't deserve hit. I go through the front door, ahead of Loujean, looking back at her on the boardwalk. She reaches out to touch a flower on the big bouquet by the door and the petals fall off in her hand.

That sets me off. I go to crying, turn toward my chair, and see Rosanne's dozing in it. I go over to the casket and pick up the curtain over Louella's young-looking face. "I'm sorry," I whisper. I take off her right glove and see the old hand that changed my babies, that cooked my food, and cleaned my mess. I love her hand to my cheek, put the glove back on.

I look back and see Loujean come through the door and hand Rosanne her fur wrop. "Go on over yonder," Loujean says to her, "and sleep with Aunt Annie Bell."

So sleepy-eyed she looks drunk, Rosanne drags the wrop across the floor to the couch and wedges in next to Annie Bell, hugging up in her fur like a big wharf rat.

Loujean comes over and puts her arm about my shoulder. I snivel, wipe my nose on my arm, and let Louella's hand go back to hits place on her middle. Loujean fixes the curtain over Louella's face and helps me to my chair and covers me up.

I'm old, older than Louella is and her dead. "The fire's out," I say.

PART THREE

Alamand

When I seen what Earl was up to on the bridge, I grabbed holt of his shirttail and dove off with him, not never turning loose till we drove into the water like picks in ice. Went down together, come up together, paddling off under the bridge to watch everybody else bailing in and dodging shots. Then we swum on out to the east bank and laid low while Boss Purvis made one last sweep across the water with the light, then got in his truck.

"I won't forget y'all!" he hollered before he crunk up and headed out.

We knowed he wouldn't.

I weren't worried about myself—not that I'm all that brave—since I weren't officially hired and I might not even be around for Buster and them to catch. I was worried about the rest of them. Specially Earl. He'd got hisself in debt to Buster and them—the county—and didn't even know for how much. Worst kind of debt, he said. He told me all that while we tromped through the woods, him following the stars, north-northeast, and me following him, clothes froze to our bodies like hardened rubber. He didn't say so, but I figgered the debt was for a good cause: Loujean. Up to now, he hadn't been making no headway with her. But big-hearted as Earl is, he'd probably have done it anyhow. Either way, I figgered everybody would be going to Mama's funeral come Sunday evening.

When we get back to Cornerville, nothing won't do Earl but for us to stand around freezing on the banks of Troublesome Creek till daylight, or till Buck and Pee Wee come loafing in. *If* they come in, as Earl said.

We watch the old man and Sonia Lee come up in a big black car, Loujean setting on the boardwalk, looking at the flowers. Looks like flowers is growing through the cracks of the boards, from one lit window to the other.

"What's all them flowers for?" I whisper to Earl.

"For the funeral," he says, peeping out from a tangle of dead bullous vines. "Shh!"

I try not to talk. "Whose car is that?" I say in his ear.

He shrugs.

I prop on his shoulder, watching. "What's Loujean up to?"

He shrugs, looks at me, then goes back to listening with one ear tuned in to the house.

In a while, the old man and Loujean go inside and Sonia Lee comes strolling down the creek dip, right past us. We iron ourselves to the trunk of a sweetgum, quit breathing. When we can't hear her shoes padding on the pavement no more, I slide down and rare back against the tree trunk to rest. I'm just getting warmed up, dozing off, when Earl takes a notion to peep through the back window of the house. "Check and see if Pee Wee and Buck might of beat us in," he says.

"Why don't we just go on inside?" My teeth are snapping at my tongue, my hair is iced.

"Dang, man!" he says. "We don't want to scare nobody in case they ain't in." He shoves off from the sweetgum, so I get up and follow him up the bank, toward the light lacing through the firewood on the scaffold.

We climb up on the boardwalk at the back, feeling our way through the cold flowers to the window. Piece by piece, we unload the wood from the scaffold till we get to where we can see through the gaping rose curtains. He looks in, holding his breath, then steps back for me to look.

I see the old man setting in his chair staring over at the corner where they've left a lamp burning. I peep around to see what he's looking at, and there's a casket. Has to be Mama. I can't see her, but I picture her just like Aunt Becky when she lay a corpse: waxy square face bogged in the puffy sleeves of her blue-figgerdy dress where her arms are locked overhead. Gray hair skint back in a bun. I know Mama don't look nothing like Aunt Becky, but she's the closest person I know dead to gauge it by. But it's the old man I'm most interested in. I ain't never seen him looking at Mama that long or with that much feeling.

The baby's crying. Loujean's standing over her on the bed. On the couch, at the foot of the bed, two fat ladies is sprawled out, wrapped in furs, sleeping with their mouths open. I know one of them is Aunt Annie Bell from Etlanna. She come to see us once when I was little and blamed me for wiping my nose on her towel. I didn't. I was just smelling since it was fluffy and sweet and our towels was stiff and sour. But I did grab her Kodak down off the table and accidentally mashed the button, setting off a flash like lightning, blinding me. When she got home and wrote back to Mama, she sent a close-up picture of my face: shocked eyes, mouth wide with two front teeth missing, the top of my head cut off. "Keep this if you want to," Aunt Annie Bell wrote. "He wouldn't own up to wiping his nose on my towel, but this time I caught him in the act." Mama stuck the picture in the frame of the dresser mirror, where it freezes me forever caught in the act.

"I bet you that's Aunt Annie Bell's car out front," I whisper to Earl.

"Shh!" he says, dancing and slinging his hands.

We stack the wood back on the scaffold, piece by piece, then tip off the boardwalk and down the creek slope to the dark woods, searching out the same old sweetgum like it's home now.

"I figger they're dead, Alamand," Earl says low. "Drownded or shot one."

"Naw," I say and mean it: Buck and Pee Wee both is blood Scurvys, and ain't no Scurvy I ever knowed of died under fifty. Except me. I have a feeling I died in that well five years ago and am fixing to find out.

Come daybreak, I'm half dozing, getting numb, peering out through the trees to where the sun is flaring the east sky. Looks like a strip of violet silk's been hung behind the church steeple, and I wish I had paint to dob on the sky of Aunt Becky's walls. Earl is standing up over where I'm setting against the gum tree, like standing up and tensing's gone make Pee Wee and Buck come on home. Ain't no way to go back and search the woods for them—I own up

I'm glad—since we don't know where they might of swum out of the river at, or even if they swum out of the river. And if they did, we don't know if they'll have the nerve to come back to Cornerville with Buster on the lookout for them.

Setting there, with Earl standing watch, I see the morning come and think how they ain't nobody I'd ruther be close to than Earl on what could be my last Sunday morning. I can smell his cold clothes, like frost on wood, and feel the seep of his blood heat, and I wish I could draw feelings. I wonder how he can care more about Buck and Pee Wee coming in than he does about going inside and getting warm; I don't know that kind of love. I can draw love easier than I can feel it, like I done yesterday when I drawed Earl in front of the telephone booth. I set straight up, knowing how I'll fix him more like he really is when I get back to Aunt Becky's.

"I hear something," he says, sucking in his breath. His square face looks like some youngun's cut it out of a book before coloring it.

I stand up and gaze with him at the house, coming clear in the daylight, at the flowers taking on color and waving as the wind picks up. Clouds smudge the dawning sky. It's warming up, fixing to rain. "Look yonder between the house and the post office," says Earl. "Who's that?"

I look down the alley of frost-nipped brown grass and see Pee Wee straggling toward the back door, gazing about, then dodging inside.

"Where's Buck?" Earl says to hisself.

"Aw, don't worry bout Buck," I say. "He's like the old man, you couldn't kill him with a stick."

"Sometimes I don't know about you, Alamand," says Earl.

He don't mean it; he does know about me. Better than anybody, now Aunt Becky's gone. He knows I'm lost, don't belong out in the real world, that the world for me is the one I make up. I need to be there now. Mama always said I was special since I was born with a double veil. Today's February twenty-third, 1960, my fifteenth birthday.

Still Earl watches the house, while I watch over the top of the house, the cold heater pipe and then the sun melting like a dip of mayhaw jelly behind the batting of white clouds. The church bell rings *ding ding ding* over the woods, and in the creek bottom goes *day day day*.

I didn't draw the bell—I sit up—just the steeple. I never noticed the bell before, even hearing it every Sunday went by for fifteen years, all I'd picked up on was the steeple. That eats at me. If there's a steeple, there's a bell, if there's a bell, it'll ring.

"There he is." Earl laughs and wipes his hand down his face, like worry is mud. I look up the alley and see Buck dragging up like a dog that's been out running deer all night: starved looking, wore out, asleep on his feet.

The tree behind Earl has woody vines growing clock-wise up the trunk—I need to hang on to that—like time. He's got on a muddy plaid work shirt, too short in the sleeves; looks like the same one he had on a few summers back when I went to stay with him in Tarver, about five miles east of Cornerville. Earl was always looking for something to get into; I was looking for some sign that I was normal. Earl would put my mind right at ease. He picked his nose and cut up in church, jacked off regular.

The same youngun that a few years before Aunt Neecy and Uncle Jim—not my real aunt and uncle—called a blessing from the Lord in their old age turned into a curse from the devil to send them to their grave. Half the time they walked around in a deep study and you knowed they was trying to figger out what went wrong—not what to do about Earl, since it wadn't in their power to do nothing with Earl. His mama would pray a lot and his old man would gripe and try to put him to work in the gum woods Uncle Jim oversaw for one of the big timber companies.

Put both of us to work, dipping gum, that summer. Up at first light and dragging to the eating table, then out with Uncle Jim to open up the commissary before he took us to the woods.

We'd been up all night, two nights running, traipsing the dark railroad tracks, looking for a spook Earl claimed to have seen. Said he'd spied a ball of light floating down the tracks from where a train had hit and kilt some gal before either of us was born. Reaching crosstie to crosstie with stretched steps, to keep from crunching in the gravel, we'd listen to one another's breathing and watch for that ball of fire. But all I seen was a knot of lightning bugs. It was his spook, not mine, and that's how come I couldn't see it.

Setting on the commissary doorsteps, waiting for Uncle Jim to finish furnishing the gum hands with sardines, soda crackers, and R.C. Colas to take to the woods, we'd listen to the grasshoppers click in the singed strips of grass along the railroad tracks where twice a day since forever the trains had slipped by. His old man was study griping inside the commissary.

"He's gone get a stick to us," I said to Earl.

"Naw," he said, trying to act like a big shot. He was fiddling with a squirt bottle of tree acid one of the hands had set on the dirt by the doorsteps. Everywhere you looked was damp gray dirt, now and then giving way to patches of dog fennels and wire grass and cat-claw briers, all closed in by the pinewoods either side of the hardroad going east to Fargo and west to Cornerville. The onliest color around was Aunt Neecy's red frame house across the tracks, the same oxblood shoe-polish color of the creosote crossties. In the heat of the day, you could smell creosote like cough medicine.

Uncle Jim followed the last hand out of the commissary and moped down the doorsteps between us. Just stood there, his green work pants bagging in the seat. He gazed up and down the railroad tracks, motioning back at Earl to let's go. Earl stood up with the squirt bottle of tree acid and stepped behind the old man to the railroad track, lifted it, and squirted the seat of his pants, then dropped the bottle into a healthy crop of dog fennels.

Before the old man got across the tracks, the seat of his pants was eat out and his flat, white backend was shining.

Up till then, Uncle Jim'd been going light on us, letting us work the stand of timber around the house in Tarver. Then he loaded us up on the back of the company pickup and drove us to the heart of the pinewoods to work with the turpentine hands. In my opinion, the prank wadn't worth it. It was to Earl.

That's when I come to know old Lucious, out there in the turpentine woods. He went to talking fast and proper, throwing in a few made-up words, claiming he was African. Me nor Earl neither one wadn't that dumb.

"You just a plain old Georgia bluegum," Earl told him. He drizzled the warm tar out of a clay pot to his dip bucket.

For something to do, I went down the pine row to empty my empty tar bucket in the barrel, gazing up the line of pines that looked like reached as far as the railroad tracks. When I got back they was still quarreling. Now Lucious was a African prince. Weren't long before I got to believing what he was saying. He didn't sound like the other gum hands, was using big words seemed like I'd read somewhere.

"Ain't nothing but a gum nigger." Earl sidled up to me and wiped his tarry hands on his dungarees. We hadn't been out there but maybe two hours, and we'd been knocking off work gradual for the past hour and a half.

Lucious, dumping gum from the clay cups bracketed to the pines, come walking toward us, swift and sure with his head high. Tall and strong, his two front teeth was gold. When he smiled, like he was doing now, you got just a glimpse of them, just enough to let you know they was real gold.

I was itching to draw him, but not just him, who he was: a African prince, not a turpentine nigger. I wanted to know him, to see what he saw, to believe in him, like Jesus. I didn't care so much if he was real or phony, as long as I could make him what I wanted him to be, and I wanted him to be a African prince. Earl wanted him to be a turpentine nigger.

Wadn't long before Lucious towed us off to watch him

plant what he called his "garden." Us done wore out before the mean sun sneaked overhead, we set out behind him to a clearing in the pines and watched as he raked out a spot in the dead straw with a forked limb. He banked the straw in a circle, the black dirt rich with rotted straw and stringy roots.

Then he started chanting—not like they do at the colored church, but a low throaty chant like he was under some spell—and took a fistful of black-eyed peas from his pockets and started sowing and dancing them into the dirt. He never looked at us, just up through the pines at the sun showering down in smoky streaks. Of a sudden, he got quiet, real quiet, so we did too. He dashed to a pine tree, shimmied up, and broke a live branch, slid down with a dreamy look—a face that could be twenty years old or fifty years old, smooth skin shrunk over blade cheekbones, but thready red eyes. He went to beating at the seeds on the dirt, circling and packing, stood tall, and put his hands on his hips and shined his teeth up at the sun that beat down on him every day. We could smell him, fishy strong and tarry, a smell that stayed in our noses even after he got done and strode back to his tar bucket and went to work.

"He's a real African prince," I said, watching him swagger off down the pine row.

"You'll believe anything!" Earl said.

But I think he believed it too.

Later that summer, we come up on old Lucious making fun of us to the other gum hands. "I sho put a fooling on them whiteboys," he said, laughing. Now he was just a plain old gum nigger. I was as disappointed as I was when I found out that the Santy Claus at church wore a strap-on cotton beard. Earl set out to get even with old Lucious, told Uncle Jim we caught him pissing in our drinking water. Uncle Jim chunked the jug out in the woods, and old Lucious out of the woods. And that's when old Lucious took to his rocking chair in Cornerville.

Now I look at Earl standing here on Troublesome Creek on a Sunday morning and know he's a different Earl, a man who can dabble around in a dream—his or somebody else's—but still keep his feet solid on the ground. This Earl, growing arms too long for his shirt-sleeves, is done with boy stuff. This Earl might bungle up trying to help somebody, but he ain't gone go out of his way to hurt nobody.

Buck

— — — — — — — — — — — — —I come busting through
the back door, not looking for nobody to be here but
Loujean and the baby—maybe the old man—and walk
into a kitchen full of women. Through the door to the living room, I see the casket and flowers, and I know some
angel of mercy's been to the undertaker with a bundle. But
don't seem like the most important thing right now; much
as I hate to say it, making shore we ain't gone have
another funeral on our hands is what's important.

I brush my hair back and hike up my muddy pants, trying to look decent, then pass on through the kitchen,
speaking to all the ladies, but my eyes is set on the casket
in the living room. Looks like sunshine. I run into Loujean
with the baby on her shoulder, coming around the bed.

"Hey," I say, backing her to the corner between the bed
and the bathroom door, "you seen Earl and them around?"

"Pee Wee," she says and shifts the baby to her other
shoulder, bless her heart. She nods at the bathroom door.
"What's wrong?" she says, curling her freckled forehead
and looking me over: ripped britches and shirt, scratched

hands, water squishing in my brogans. And I can tell she's done been through the same thing with Pee Wee. Her face looks too worried up for a young girl's. Don't nobody else act like I look all that strange, so I figger Pee Wee's done broke them in. Besides, our name ain't all that good around here. We normally get to cutting up on a Saturday night, and our neighbors act like they don't notice: Sunday morning'll come and we'll settle down; Monday morning, we'll be hard at work, like we're going through the motions just to get to another Saturday-night fight.

I aim to straighten this bunch out.

Just for Mama, I for one ain't gone make no fuss this morning. I'm too happy to see her home and everything worked out. Well, some of it anyhow. My face burns thinking about the other. Us boys is gone have to make ourselfs scarce around Cornerville, or leave, one. I swallow hard and listen for Pee Wee through the bathroom door. I hear water running, smell sulfur. I knock.

"Pee Wee?" I call.

Somebody bumps me from behind, then Cousin Winston goes around me and sprawls face-down on the bed. I didn't know he was home from the pen.

The bathroom door rattles, opens, and Pee Wee stands scrubbing his neck with a towel. His hairless caved chest is slick yellow, his eyewhites scribbled with red.

"You seen Earl and Alamand anywheres?" I ask him.

He scrubs his face with the towel, drops it, and turns toward the mud-ringed sink. "Out yonder at the creek," he says and spraddles his legs and stoops to look in the broke mirror over the sink while he combs his hair. "Seen 'em when I come up," he adds.

Feels like a binder's been took off my chest. "They look all right?"

"Yep." He parts his wet brown hair. "For two fellers had to jump off a river bridge, they do."

"What about you?"

He quits combing his hair, feet still planted with his stick legs apart, and glares at me with them dead brown eyes. "What you care?" he says.

He's got every right to be mad at me. It hits me that we went to all that trouble and danger to get the money to put Mama away and somebody done took care of it. Makes me kind of mad, which don't make no sense. I don't expect it to, life's like that.

"Who put up the money for Mama?" I say, hearing Loujean slipping up behind me to eavesdrop with the baby squalling like a safepin's sticking in her.

"Do it matter?" says Pee Wee. He bounces the comb in the sink and shoves around me in the doorway.

A woman comes around me from behind and stands just inside the bathroom. "You boys will have to go elsewhere to talk over your meanness," she says. "I've got to freshen up in this pigsty."

Aunt Annie Bell, looking drooped as a cloth flower. Her curls is limp, her black dress twisted. I wonder who called her up. I don't speak, but I could hug her neck for coming and taking care of Mama's funeral arrangements. If she did. I look at the old scaling snakeskin case she's toting and doubt it. The two times I seen her in my life, she looked poor but acted rich. I think it's the way she talks proper and pushes everybody around that makes her seem rich. But I owe her if she's the one traded with the undertaker.

I turn around and start to tell Pee Wee to lets us treat her nice, for Mama's sake—we can give her a proper funeral now—but he's gone. Loujean's standing by the bed with the baby, watching Aunt Annie Bell kick dirty clothes out the bathroom door before she slams it. I don't believe it was her made the funeral arrangements.

"How'd you swing it, Old Man?" I say, just me and him setting at the eating table while everybody wanders from the kitchen to the living room and back again.

"I hain't done hit." He swigs black Luzianne from a saucer, pours more from his cracked white cup, and glances to his right at the casket. "I got a good notion they did hit." He nods at the bathroom where Aunt Annie Bell's still "freshening up" and fussing with Aunt Rosanne in the doorway.

Loujean's on the bed tending to the baby, whose crying's getting to be just a background racket like the frogs at the creek.

"You didn't go a-begging Buster, did you?" the old man says to me.

I take a sip of coffee and clear my throat. I'm so stove up lifting the cup makes my right shoulder ache. "Ain't none of my doings," I say. I'm relieved, but I want to know who to credit before I get too relieved. Maybe the old man's thinking that too. Flowers is high and rank in the dim room. The Frigidaire is sweating, it's so muggy. The coffee makes my stomach gripe, that and fear. Buster won't let me off light this time, but like they say, they's safety in numbers. He'll have to bear down on all of us boys.

One of the church ladies is leaving through the front

door; another one comes in carrying a angel food cake and sets it on the crowded table. She speaks. We speak. Then we set there mulling it all over like business while she tips to the casket, then to the kitchen. The old man's side of the family floats in and out like flies: quiet, set aside, abiding.

Alamand and Earl's done come in and gone again, and they didn't look no worse than me and Pee Wee. If it hadn't been for Earl, I could be dragging a cement block on the floor of Little River this morning. Or in jail, or rich. Still, I'm beholding. I couldn't say nothing to him in front of everybody, but I nodded to him in the kitchen. He nodded back, then ducked out the door behind Alamand. I still wonder how come him to get mixed up with Buster.

Loujean eases past the table with the baby in her arms and sets down behind us in the rocker by the cold heater. She walks the rocker around so that her back is to us, then starts feeding the baby from a suck bottle. I watch her rock, listen to the floor joists squawking. I figger she's put out with me and the old man for cutting out on the wake.

The old man, on my right, seems too solemn. I can't think about him and Loujean and everything else; I'm too wore out. I brace my arms on the table and lay my head on them, and before I can blink, I feel, see, the hair raise on my arms. I set up. I know who paid the undertaker, how come Earl to be mixed up with Buster, and it's like being God up above knowing everything and too much. I knock my cup over and mop up the coffee with my shirt sleeve. The old man looks at me. I light a cigarette and my hands is shaking.

"It was Earl," I say low.

The old man leans toward me—"Say what?" Looks like he's listening with his melty green eyes.

"Earl paid the undertaker."

"Naw." Old Man rares back, grinning at one of the ladies on her way to the kitchen.

"He's got in with Buster," I say, like I'm thinking out loud, talking low and not holding nothing back. Every sentence or so, the old man says, "Huh?" and I have to speak up and worry about somebody hearing. "They'll kill him," I say. "Look at all these flowers, that casket. He must owe them . . . ain't no tellings how much."

"Naw," says the old man, tapping the tabletop with his bulb knuckles. He sets to one side with his sharp knees crossed, swinging one foot, then places them both flat on the floor. Watching everybody in the room but me. I know he's listening though.

I decide to pump Earl up to be a hero, knowing Loujean's listening, but then again I ain't so sure he's not. "The onliest thing saved me and Pee Wee last night was Earl thinking fast and jumping in the river first to throw Boss Purvis off track," I say.

"Naw!" the old man says.

"Yes," says Loujean, still with her back to us. "He went in debt to Buster for me. He did it." We all get still, waiting for a drove of Scurvys to spirit through the room and out the front door.

"Buster and them'll kill him," Loujean says, rocking and staring at the baby sleeping in her arms with the nipple in its mouth. "Won't they, Buck?"

"Unless we can come up with a miracle they might." I know it'll take at least that: dangerous enough bootlegging and getting paid afterwards, but to get paid before you go to bootlegging, then running out on them, you can kiss your ass goodbye.

Aunt Rosanne and Aunt Annie Bell come prancing through the room with their high heels clicking—don't even look at us—go to the casket to check on Mama and prance back through to the kitchen.

Loujean waits till they're gone, then says, "Tell Buster Aunt Annie Bell's a special agent for the GBI, and if he does anything to Earl, she'll uncover his whole shine operation."

"A GBI agent?" I wheel my chair around and look at the side of Loujean's face, a little smile working at the hinge of her thin lips. "She is?" I say.

"She ain't, far as I know," says Loujean. "But she's a secretary in the GBI office in Etlanna. Can't hurt stretching it a little."

"Naw," I say, watching the old man's eyes get greener.

He gets up and goes to the heater, holding his hands over it like he's warming. Grinning with his red gums shining.

"Buster's running for county commissioner again, you know?" says Loujean.

"He won't do nothing to us till after the funeral then," I say. "You ever know Buster to miss a chance to lectioneer at a funeral. He'll want everybody to think he's the one got Mama put away."

Aunt Annie Bell teeters back into the room, to the table this time, and reaches under the foil cover of a plate and draws out a sweet roll with her long red nails.

"Naw," I say, watching her nibble the roll. "Who'd believe it?"

"Buster might," says Loujean.

"Somebody with a bad grudge against him might could drop a hint and . . ." I drop what I'm saying like a rat for the old hawk at the heater to pick up in the field he's working.

Earl

— — — — — — — — — — — When I fell head over heels for Loujean, I want to shacking up in Buster's old store, bad as it sounds, to sleep close to Loujean: a bed of feed sacks, like a rat nest, next to the wall dividing the store from the Scurvy house and the head of Loujean's bed. Oh Lord!

Not all the time. Sometimes, to make it look good, I go to my mama's in Tarver. But most of the time, I won't lie, I'm right here listening out in case Loujean wants or needs something, so I can get it for her before she even knows she wants or needs it. Which is fast wearing me out, I won't lie.

Now, laying here, staring at the faded red writing— COCA-COLA—on the wood crates stacked one, two, three by my nest, and my good yellow shirt on a wire hanger hooked to the top, I listen to the jabbering and heel clicks other side of the wall and try to sleep. But when I close my eyes, the crates with COCA-COLA on them and my yellow shirt are printed on the gray-grainy backsides of my eyelids. With Buster's sharp green eyes peeping over the crates. Oh Lord!

Yes sir, I jimmied the lock on this door. But I ain't messed with nothing. Yes sir, I bailed out on you after you went to the undertaker and made Loujean's mama's funeral arrangments for me. And I'd do it again.

Yes sir, Buster, I'm about as lowdown as you are. I'm getting there.

Other side of the wall, the baby's crying and I picture Loujean rocking her before the cold heater, and I'm sorry for her, real sad, but I can't say as I'm in love with her no more, but I love her. Just like I love Alamand, like I love Jesus.

I feel sleep tingling in my head, fixing to come, and wonder what'll happen if Loujean finds out I'm the one made the funeral arrangements. If she'll fall in love with me and want to marry me, she's so beholding. And then I picture Buster's eyes again and feel safe.

Alamand

Sunday mornings in Cornerville's got that shutdown feeling to them right after the church bell rings, specially when it's clouding up to rain. The sky is like a upside-down bowl of dirty soapsuds. Everybody ain't in church is sleeping late or slow getting going, and I'm walking in amongst them, like God in the morning in the Garden of Eden. It's that peaceful, but it's lonesome too, waiting on the rain. Waiting on everybody to get stirring. I like it though. I like the damp dirt sticking to my shoes, my soft walking; the birds tweeting in the still trees, the air dead. When it's like this, you can't tell summer from winter, just one even season—Before Rain. No shadows. No smell till the rain comes, then it's like fresh-dug peanuts.

I can't draw sounds and smells anyhow.

It's a good day for drawing, but I feel too billous from being up all night. That bothers me. If I lay down to sleep, I might not get up in time to fix my picture, and it's bearing down on me. One minute, it's so important I can't stand it; the next minute, it ain't worth a toot. I can't afford to waste such a blank-even day. But if I try to draw now, I won't be no good. Here I am with two good pencils, plenty of eraser on both of them, and can't keep them out of my mouth; the day's just about as good as they get, and nobody won't be in my way, and what do I do but go and get billous?

When I get to Aunt Becky's, I'll just have to lay down and hope I can get back up in time. I've got till three o'clock to draw, then I got to go to Mama's funeral at the little church I'm walking past. It's around nine now, and if I sleep till ten, I'll have a good five hours' drawing time.

My heart's not in it no more, but sometimes when I lay down it comes to me.

I do hate to have to go back and fix something I've done. But there it is on a wall this time, for all the world to see. I don't guess I could erase the whole thing; maybe I could paint over it. Buster'll probably tear Aunt Becky's house down anyhow, or more like him, use it for a pack-house. Might even turn it into a tobacco packhouse. Then everybody unstringing the cooked tobacco will see I wadn't never no hand to draw—perfect like the picture is, it ain't real-looking. And what was it I might have put there, I don't want the world to see?

I go to walking, good and woke up.

Loujean

_ _ _ _ _ _ _ _ _ _ _ **B**y two o'clock, a sprinkling rain sets in for the day, just enough to keep dirt tracking in the house.

The hearse and flower van comes and they load up the casket and flowers. The house looks empty, like the time Buster made us move out. Next day, the old man moved us right back in—cookstove and all—in a wheelbar. I don't know how he got Buster to let us move back, since we didn't pay the rent—that's men's doings. Most of the time, I just hear stuff, but like Mama don't have time to dwell on it. Stuff like her saying Alamand was born with a double veil. I don't know what that means, but it sounds pretty. You can bet it ain't. If I wanted to understand it, I'd have to know more about having babies than I do. I know all I want to know, and it don't seem all that romantic.

I won't marry Earl. I'll do him and myself a favor. He's been used enough.

In my heart, I know Buster won't kill him since nobody around Cornerville don't kill nobody, they just make like they might. But I do hate to end up a old maid, and have everybody around here think something's wrong with me. The baby's mine now. I dress her in a hand-smocked pink gown from Miss Amaretta and bundle her in a blanket. She's sleeping so she can stay up tonight. I pick her up and follow Aunt Rosanne and Aunt Annie Bell out to their car parked right behind the hearse. The post truck is parked behind Aunt Annie Bell's car, with Buck and them scrunched together and scooched low: Buck under the steering wheel and Pee Wee setting by the other door, arms crooked in the open windows; and between them, Earl in his yellow shirt and the old man, sharp face the shade of beef tallow . . . the old man, who looks like but don't seem like the same man said, Me and your mommer's done with one another, y'all do what you want to about hit. Other cars and trucks with people setting ready for what my aunts call "the procession" is lined up along the courthouse square.

My aunts carry big black umbrellas to match their frocks and car, which looks about ten times worse with the rain streaking dust down the bunged-up side. The right mirror is dangling like a loose tooth. They pitched a fit when they looked out this morning and seen it; Aunt Annie Bell threatened to call up the law. Everybody acted like they didn't know what happened, but the old man said he seen a transfer truck plow into it. Course they didn't believe that for a minute, but they wadn't about to cramp their style by getting nothing going with the law and it right here time for them to show off at the funeral. Besides, they needed all morning to get theirselfs together, and getting the law into it would of took too much time. They ain't overed it though: I just heared Aunt Rosanne tell Aunt Annie Bell that the best way to draw attention to the car's condition is to keep harping on it. That shut her up.

They do look funny now, all gussied up and crawling into the front of this bunged-up car. I start to get in the back seat and hear one of the neighbor women say to another one, "Rosanne's holding up good, ain't she?" and I wonder if they mean because of her age or her grieving over Mama.

I got a good notion Alamand's off drawing somewhere and forgot what time it is. He might make it to the funeral, and he might not. He might just wander up on the church house while he's out roaming the quarters, or he might show up later and hate hisself for missing it. Nobody won't get mad with him; everybody loves him. They all know he's touched. Maybe him being born with a double veil is how come he's always walking around in a daze, like his eyes is turned around looking inside his head.

Sheriff Amos drives up the cement slope in front of the house, blue lights slicing the rainy gray air, and leads the hearse out on 129, us all following and circling back to the crossing where Deputy Saul stands with his cap over his heart. We turn east along 94 and the cars and trucks at the courtyard dribble in behind the family. I swallow around the lump in my throat, watching Mama's shiny casket through the back window of the black hearse. I don't feel sad, just tired and worried: How am I gone take care of this baby? Here I am, getting what I wanted more than anything—Mama's funeral, the baby left to me now—and I'm still not happy. Nobody pro'bly wouldn't have my sister, crying like she does three-fourths of the time. She's

like a siren. I couldn't of pinched her and made her cry
no louder. Now I'm stuck with her. I look down at Joy's
sweet peach head and feel guilty; she didn't ask to be born.
Joyful Noise. Some joyful noise! "I'd take her, sugarplum,"
Aunt Inez said this morning, "but I got all I can do to look
out for me and mine." Cousin Winston just got out of the
pen for stealing hogs—Buster's hogs. If somebody was to
kill Buster, the law would have a time trying to study up
who done it.

At the red brick schoolhouse, Aunt Annie Bell turns
off behind the hearse, tires singing on the gravel shoulders
and vapors steaming from the blacktop like hell's right up
under Cornerville.

"That old schoolhouse sure brings back the memories,"
Aunt Rosanne says and sets straight. Ever since she got in
the car, she's been scrubbing at a matted place on her fur
where something sticky's been spilled on it, I guess.

"Don't remind me about those days," says Aunt Annie
Bell.

I wonder if she means because life then was so good,
but decide she don't want to be reminded of her school
days because she thinks she's overcome what she was then.

"Hicks!" she says. "Getting an education has been a
regular quest."

They don't act like I'm even in the car. We go on past
the smoking tree behind the schoolhouse and up the
straightaway, to the horseshoe curve of the quarters, where
a runty little colored boy stands watching all the cars pass.

"Look at that little pickaninny!" Aunt Rosanne waves
at the boy like she's in a parade. Aunt Annie Bell clicks
her tongue, "Nck nck nck," driving with one fat hand on

the wheel and the other laid across the top of the front seat. "Looks like we could have had the funeral at that sweet little Methodist Church," she says.

You don't get better when you go off to make something out of yourself, I think, you just learn how to say stuff a different way. They look overfed and wore-out, more wore-out than Mama was. She could always find something to look forward to: in summer, she'd look for fall, and in winter, she'd look for spring, wild flowers, and a new baby. All my aunts have to look forward to is their next meal.

Setting at the house this morning, talking about where-all they been, they always ended up talking about "eating out." Key West—lime pie; West Virginia—rabbit stew; Lookout Mountain—coconut cream pie; Michigan—tomato pudding. Setting wall-eyed over in one corner, Cousin Winston perked up at the mention of tomato pudding. Aunt Annie Bell told him you have to "cultivate a taste for it."

I picture them gallivanting around some hotel at sunset, grumbling right after they eat, too full to eat another mouthful, trying to come up with something to do till they can eat again. I bet it costs more in a month's time to keep up one of them than it does to feed our whole bunch.

I'll be glad when they leave. I hold the baby close on the next curve, coming up on the one-room church with its side dressing of cedar trees that scrub the white blocks green. I can smell the damp dirt outside in the quarters, like sweaty socks. A couple of fice dogs run after the car tires; a fat mama dog with droopy tits waddles out from under one of the shanty porches, and Aunt Annie Bell gets started on a speech about "neutering." I love words; I'll keep that one.

Cars and trucks are already parked both sides of the muddy road and in the church yard, with a space left in front for the hearse and guess who? Buster's blue truck with the camper top is set so that the hearse has to pull up to his back bumper to get close to the door. Aunt Annie Bell stops her car behind the hearse, clears her throat, and gathers up her fat black patent-leather pocketbook. Then she slides her stole around her shoulders and her nylony blond curls bog into the fur.

We step out to the crowd of waiting neighbors, all watching the hearse and my aunts, who step to one side of the stoop and pose under black umbrellas. They look tall and bright—black silk, patent leather, diamonds, and furs—all shine.

"There's your old sweetheart." Aunt Rosanne elbows Aunt Annie Bell in the ribs and nods toward Buster, who is standing at the rear of the hearse with the pallbearers.

He takes one last puff on his cigarette, drops it, and mashes it with the toe of his black lectioneering shoe. He's got on his good black suit, faded to the sun-bleached shade of buzzard wings. On his right lapel, he's got a round button says BUSTER FOR COMMISSION about the size of a silver dollar.

"Great God!" Aunt Rosanne whispers to Aunt Annie Bell. "Buster's running for state commissioner."

"County commissioner," corrects Aunt Annie Bell. Buck, Earl, Pee Wee, and the old man get out of the post truck and amble around the other side of Aunt Annie Bell's car. The old man heads toward the hearse, eyes on

Buster, eyes on the casket. The boys hang back like they're checking Aunt Annie Bell's tires. Pulling up behind the post truck, Uncle Albert's pieced-together brown pickup is loaded with younguns he had to pull out of the creek bed, fussing cause they wanted to stay and play. Car doors snib open and clap shut behind the post truck, all the way to the curve of the quarters. The undertaker starts toward the stoop, a fixed smile on his gray face, followed by the pall-bearers with the casket.

Buster spies my aunts, steps to one side, and sticks out his paw to shake. "Y'all just as pretty as ever," he says, looking right at Aunt Annie Bell's heart diamond on her throat, which is where the top of his head comes up to.

She might not know it, but she's about thirty years too old to suit Buster's taste. He likes em young, real young. I can tell my aunts thinks he's the one behind getting Mama put away, and I can tell he wants them to think that. Course I know he knows it was Earl done it, but either my aunts or Buster one will get public credit.

The old man struts around Buster and up to the cas-ket, about halfway between the hearse and the stoop. I think he's up to something, the way he's been eyeing Buster. For once, I hope he is, but I hope he'll wait till after the funeral. He reaches out and wipes beads of rain from the casket, and I figger he'll wait. When the old man's side of the family gathers at the stoop, I get closed in by them (you can go for months without seeing hide nor hair of a Scurvy, but let a funeral come up . . .). Somebody behind us grunts, then a sliding thud, and I peep out to see Buster laying broadside in the mud. The crowd mumbles and scrambles, circling him, and when they back off I see

Earl helping him up, brushing mud off Buster's buzzard-black suit. Earl looks like he's forgot to be scared, is just doing what comes natural. Old Man, standing next to Buster, is grinning, twisting, looking off at the rain falling on the dead pasture across the road.

Earl is now toting the casket with the pallbearers through the door, up the aisle, while Buster, ruffled as a chicken, walks stiff alongside. Aunt Rosanne and Aunt Annie Bell toddle on in behind the casket. Aunt Annie Bell's got a white ironed handkerchief balled over her mouth. The boys come in behind them and I step out of the crowd and walk with them.

I would like to have had a little piano music, but the Church of Sinners don't believe in music. I wouldn't give Aunt Annie Bell the satisfaction of knowing it, but the Methodist Church would have been my pick too. I love the bells. When they ring on Sunday mornings and evenings, it's like the air comes alive. Close to the house as the Methodist Church is, Mama never went there. Never said how come, but I figgered she felt more at ease in this little block church behind the quarters, where just poor white people go. I bet if the coloreds took a notion to build them a church in the heart of Cornerville, the Ku Klux Klan would burn it down, but poor whites and coloreds is got a lot in common. Going to school, you know that. Nobody, except kin, don't generally sociate with you, which is all right if you're like me and kin to about three-fourths of the county. And even at home, specially on Fridays, you get a lesson in how poor white people and coloreds is alike when the policy man from the insurance company in Valdosta stops off at your house on his way to collect in the quarters, looking to sell you life insurance (if he waits till Monday the coloreds will all be spent their paychecks on moonpies and bootleg whiskey). He left us the picture calendar of Jesus, even though we didn't buy any insurance, the same white Jesus pro'bly hanging in every house in the quarters.

Aunt Annie Bell is setting on the front pew by the window, left side, with Aunt Rosanne beside her. Pee Wee, next in line, has left a gap between him and Aunt Rosanne, so I have to set beside her or set on the second pew with the rest of the Scurvys—babies bawling, younguns talking, mamas slapping at them. Aunt Rosanne crosses her stuffed legs and her stockings whisper. Purse on her lap with her hands latched on top. Her elbows stick out and I have to lay the sleeping baby so that her head is jam-up with Pee Wee's shaking arm. I prechate him not drinking till after the funeral, but I feel sorry for him with that gnawed face, that suffering look.

I look back to see if the old man has come in and can't spot him in the packed church. The pallbearers set stiff on the other front pew, Earl and Buster in the middle, shoulder to shoulder.

"Where's the old man?" I whisper across Pee Wee to Buck.

"Ain't no tellings," he says through his teeth, eyes on the casket parked at the foot of the altar. The baby stirs and I set back, stop breathing till she settles like sand in water in my arms. Bright pink patches have popped up on her eyelids. I wonder what I've done or not done to cause that.

"Buck," I say across Pee Wee again, "you better run go see about the old man."

"He knows where we holding the funeral at," says Buck, watching the stumpy preacher with wiglike tan hair waddle up the aisle and wedge into one of the chairs on the pulpit.

Miss Lizabeth, one of the church ladies, comes to the front and starts singing "Amazing Grace," with her lashless blue eyes lifted to the low ceiling. Aunt Annie Bell squirms, shaking the hard slat pew, I guess to let us know the singing don't sound to suit her. The preacher come by the house last night and got his orders to read from the Twenty-third Psalm, then have a little piano music. When he told Aunt Annie Bell his church didn't believe in music, she put in to have the funeral at "that sweet little Methodist Church." Had Aunt Rosanne all primed at the door to dash over to the new phone booth—which they've about wore out making "business calls" since they got here—and call the Methodist preacher. It was Aunt Inez filled my aunts in on the fact that the Methodist preacher would be preaching at the Fargo church this Sunday, and no way would he let the Church of Sinners' preacher, who at that point was looking about as whipped as Aunt Rosanne, preach at the Methodist Church.

Aunt Annie Bell then said to Aunt Rosanne, "Is it my fault everything's gone awry?"

"Awry," another word I like, I'll keep, though I'll never use it.

The preacher now gets up and goes to the podium, flipping the tissue pages of his Bible, while watching the aisle. The old man comes striding across in front of us, hikes his green twill britches legs and scoots between Aunt Rosanne and Aunt Annie Bell. Buster sets forward, close-set green eyes fixed on the old man, arms crossed so that the chest of his coat pooches and his lectioneering button looks like it reads COMMISSION FOR BUSTER.

I can see the old man's sharp knee, his foot swinging, just missing Aunt Annie Bell's pumped-up calf.

"Let us pray," says the preacher.

The baby wakes up and sets right in squalling. No warm-up warning, nothing. Another baby, behind us, starts squalling too, sounds like they're singing.

"Take that baby out!" Aunt Rosanne shouts low to me.

I stand up and make it to the end of the pew, everybody standing in the middle aisle parting for me to pass, and Joy starts sucking her thumb. I start to go on out anyway, then hear the rain coming down harder. I stop about halfway up the aisle, fixing to turn, and see Buster's old blue pickup setting lopsided, right front and left rear tires flat as my heart. I doubt it was the old man tripped Buster, but I don't doubt he's let the air out of Buster's tires.

I look at Buster's wet-blond cone head, as I start back to our pew, and I wouldn't change places with him for nothing.

"Sister Louella's been a longtime friend of mine," says the preacher. "A member of this church ever since we started. Used to clean the church, teach Sunday school, whatever needed doing, and I never once heard her complain. Many's the time I set down to her table . . ."

I hope he don't tell about the old man running him off that time for eating up his "vittles." Never could understand us inviting company to eat.

"She raised a big bunch of children," the preacher goes on, "every one of them the best she knew how."

Oh, boy! Pee Wee's scooched down with a tunnel running between his back and the pew; Buck is setting straight and still. Looks like he's just now settled down long enough to realize Mama's in that casket below the pulpit. Buck was her favorite, how come he ain't left home yet. Pee Wee closes his eyes. It's all so easy when you keep your eyes shut, Pee Wee, I think. Out of all of the hell-raisers Mama's raised, he's raised the most hell. I can't see the old man, just one wore-out brogan, still now, and I think how he was as much a youngun to Mama as ery one of us. I feel guilty, since in my heart I've hated all of them at one time or another, and sometimes even hated Mama for having them. All except Alamand.

Alamand

The house is still, except for rat claws scratching on the brittle board floor. I shut the front door and they stop. I know they're still here, maybe under the bed of papers I'm standing on. I see where they've gnawed up some of my drawings to make a nest. The rats smell musty and dry, like a paperlined trunk. Old, before-time, after-time, moving now.

I'm still billous, but I don't let it get in my way. I try not to. I mope around in the mess of papers and junk and make like I'm not up to nothing, feeling my heart clawing at my ribcage like the rats are inside me, trying to scratch out.

The light in the room's a even spread of gray, and I know if I look at the walls the pencil markings will show up good. Don't look, not yet! Not with the picture perfect like it is and unreal. I act like I'm just plundering, the way anybody else would, and go on in the kitchen at the back of the house.

Rusty nails poke from the tongue-and-groove walls, unpainted heartpine that looks stained reddish-brown. No light, except for a square gray smear coming through the single pane over Aunt Becky's cook table. A piece of tobacco twine hangs from a nail by the window. The window's broke, but the string don't move. It's that still. So still I can hear that one cricket by itself, like a squeaky door hinge. I stand there and let the sound sink in till I feel easy enough. Too easy and I won't have the energy to finish my picture.

To get myself going, I start walking around the kitchen. A five-gallon lard can lays on its side; if it rolls the racket will mess me up. I walk around it, kicking at a pile of quiet rags, at the soft air and light. Doing what I do from whatever it is inside makes me do it; I don't know what and don't want to.

When I'm right, I pick up a three-legged milking stool and tote it through the door to the front room and set it against the wall where my picture started in the block of sun yesterday.

I just about get mad with myself, cause where the drawing started ain't the real beginning of the wall. Not plumb with the corner. That's okay; guess I started where I needed to. I gotta trust myself. The block of sun was where the picture should of been started, I guess. (I always tell myself little stuff like that to keep going, in case I might turn out something good by accident. I have faith that way. I try to.) But I know as good as I know my name I'm gone need that space in the corner to do what I have to do now. (I have feelings like that, and I trust them, I try to.) Sure enough, touching up the screen door of the café, where it's been tore loose, I need that space on the left moved to the right in order to add on Miss Annette's extra room she's planning to build on the south end. It's important to add the room on since that's how the café will look later, because that's her plans for the future.

I do the best I can with the space I have—must keep saying that. Looking all right to run the new room off at a angle toward the back of the café. She might like that better anyhow; keep from crowding too close to Mr. Rackard's new barbershop south of the café.

Why didn't I start this picture with the barbershop instead of the café?

I can't think that way or I'll lose interest in my drawing. Besides, I had to start somewhere, and I don't really know the barbershop. It's too new. (Don't try to make meaning from the whole thing too early or it won't mean nothing.) Wait! Wait! I draw faster, swapping off one pencil with the other, erasing, sketching in—I'm doing fine—all the way up to the telephone booth.

I get down, move the milking stool over to my right; I'm gone need it in a minute. I've got to open up 94, west to Valdosta. But first, Earl's got to be fixed. I do hate to erase his plaid shirt; plaids is hard to do, all them squares, and I used up most of my pencil lead making it yesterday. I draw him a plain shirt with lines in a patch to show it's shiny. Should be yellow, will be when the sun shines. I'll make like it till I can get me some paint.

I go on and open up 94, since opening roads is important. Now I can't wait to open up the rest of them. Slow down! Yesterday, I rushed past all the roads leading out of Cornerville, and today I can't wait to open them up. Standing off, looking at that one section of the picture, I wonder if there's not something special in that opening-

and-closing road business, but I can't afford thinking about that now. I've just got to keep moving, fixing, making . . . making it real. I breathe slow and study and erase the fade-out lines on 94 West. Draw two solid lines up higher to show the road going on, draw the river bridge and a man standing on the other side. Pee Wee. It's Pee Wee.

I feel like God.

I keep working on Pee Wee: his wide black belt, one knee bent, head down, a few loose hairs sticking up on the crown. Erase two hairs—too many, like a cartoon character. I don't want that, not here.

It's good.

And God said, That is good.

Buck

It's bad when you have to dread your own mama's funeral getting over cause you know you might face a killing.

I can't help myself—uptight the whole time just before the funeral, and now is like a time to rest, a real Sunday. If the old man don't fix it with Buster, me and Pee Wee's goners. Earl, he ain't got a prayer. And there he sets, the nut, right next to his killer. He's the kind would set down in the lectric chair and smile while they turn on the juice.

I'm sorry, Mama, for finding such peace in your funeral, but generally if I ain't working I'm running, and I had to have a break or break down one. I do thank you for nussing me and seeing to it I got good home-cooked meals and all. I'm resting with you, Mama, if that's all right, just like I used to do when I was little and you'd lay down to get off your feet and I'd snug up to you and hear your bad heart pumping while it still could. I'd lay listening for it to flutter, like you said it was doing, and hear it beat just as regular as the rain is right now. Weren't that I didn't believe you—I did—but I'd just lived so long with waiting for your heart to quit it was like I was winding up. And when it did quit, this time, mine didn't quit too like I thought it would.

I reckon I don't blame you if you was putting on; you didn't have all that many ways to get our attention. You kept me straight many a time with your bad heart. I'd be all set in my mind to make a big wad of dough illegal, and I'd picture you laying there with your heart fluttering, the blood veins in your legs sticking out, smelling sidemeat you just fried on your clothes and hair, and I wouldn't have the heart for no meanness.

You raised me right, Mama, but I'm still lacking.

Pee Wee

The Lord is my shepherd, I shall not want.
He maketh me to lie down in green pastures. . . .

If I open up my eyes, my teeth will clamp down. My jaw's done drawing. I need a drink bad. Bad as I ever needed one. And there's my own mama laying dead.

Yea, though I walk through the valley of the shadow of
death, I will fear no evil: for thou art with me. . . .

If I open up my eyes, I'll have to look at the baby that killed her, and I might love her and I don't want to. And if I do, what then? It's not that I give a hang what people think of me—I don't. But I don't know if I can just up and walk off and leave Loujean with the baby. She's mine as much as Loujean's, as much as the old man's, who ain't no old man atall, but a youngun. How can I leave him? Alamand? I need a drink.

Right here in Cornerville, I ain't able to run hog-wild and scared while I wait for the next port coming up to get drunk. Time's messed up. I set up and throw my head back; my eyes are still shut.

Thou preparest a table before me in the presence of mine enemies. . . .

I hope so Lord, I hope so.

Surely goodness and mercy shall follow me all the days of my life.

Sonia Lee's leaving. I might follow after her, and then again I might not. I'm glad I didn't kill her and mix everything up worse than it is. I can't take no more of the old man's stories, much as anything. How many times can you set and listen to the same old crap about Great-Uncle John getting the county on its feet?

Loujean

Sister Louella preached her own funeral while she was living," says the preacher, his stern gaze settling on her family.

I set up, thinking about that while listening to the colored younguns playing outside. Their laughing in the rain is like bells.

Joy wakes up and bellers out. I look at her pink round mouth and listen to the oldest noise on this old earth. A joyful noise. I don't care if she screams her lungs out, if my aunts have a hissy. Crying's how we all started, how we'll all end. And everything makes sense, coming round in a circle from being born to dying. I think how a woman makes it all start, how important I am. Like Mama, I can make a baby (not that I'm planning on it). And with every one of us—Buck, Pee Wee, Alamand, me, Joy, even as to the dead babies—Mama's died a little bit till she's all dead. But not dead as much as used up, done doing what she was put here to do, then going on to soak up the earth like a sponge. The earth where we all come from and go back to.

My aunts are shallow and dry, have made no noise.

Mama preached her own funeral through us.

Alamand

_____ I'm happy.

I get down and move my stool around the next corner and open up 129, north of Troublesome Creek.

I don't look back over everything else I drawed, but I do check the beginning to see if I opened up 129 South, to Florida. I did, and of course the spare space to the left of the café, off the corner where I started from, turned out to be necessary after all. In a minute, I'll go back and put up the city-limits signs on all the road shoulders.

God, I'm doing good!

I go on and make this sign now, so I won't forget it; and then, like dream magic, I draw three transfer trucks running north on 129, up toward the ceiling. Four would of been too many, higher than I can reach, and besides, a even number like that wouldn't look real. I want this picture real.

My heart beats faster. Sometimes it does that when I'm drawing, to let me know something good's coming up. It scares me. I try to slow down. I'm at the old store that hooks onto our house—Buster's store and the rooms we rent. (I'm losing it because of Buster.) I go on and start fixing the trees on the banks of Troublesome Creek, taller with dangling fox-grape vines. I make the vines thready, bare, curling to the dirt, since it's winter now—now while I'm drawing—and it's easier, better, to do a scene during the same season. I don't know if that tells anything about me as a artist, but it works for me. I hope it does.

God, I'm pro'bly not good atall! I'm pro'bly just crazy! I go on anyway and draw the clothesline behind the house, because now that I've started this picture on this wall, where everybody and his brother might see it, I've got to do it right.

I'm billous again. I go on making a thick gray line across the tangle of vines on the creek bank, drawing hanging shirts and frocks and britches real as I can, but feel like I'm doodling at school while the teacher's talking. It's that dern old cricket squeaking; I wish he'd go on. I know the rats are watching. I ain't heared a peep out of them, though.

Mama's under the clothesline, flapping out a shirt to hang up. I've drawed her before I realized it: big-boned, slump-shouldered, smiling, gray hair straying around her long face. I move her over, I move the whole thing over, cause of a knothole, then I move her back because the color of the wood suits her better where I drawed her in the first place.

I wish I had color, but at least I have this good pencil Loujean left on the mantelshelf at home.

I stand back and look at her and don't feel no special meaning coming out of the picture like I expected. I just try to remember to quit drawing by three for her funeral and know I don't have a watch, that the sun won't come out from behind the clouds for me to go by, and I'll have a good excuse for not going.

That's the kind of sorry person I am.

Loujean

For all the pains we went to, it does seem to me like the funeral should last a little longer; something big should come out of it. The preacher reads Mama's favorite Bible verse—"Jesus wept"—and sets down in his chair behind the pulpit. I can't recall her ever mentioning that being her favorite verse, and if Aunt Annie Bell and them wants to gripe about such a quick wrap-up, I don't blame them.

The undertaker, all in gray, strolls up the aisle and stands before the casket and raises both arms and asks the family to stay seated while everybody outside and those standing come by first to pay their last respects. His two helpers slide the yellow roses on top of the casket to the right end, then open the lid on the left end. I look over at the old man, setting forward with his gums shining, green eyes sunk in his head, and figger he's thinking about Aunt Becky, his midget sister, being buried with her arms locked overhead, about this same undertaker charging him extra for a regular-size coffin, then dunning him every month. Old Man just has to pay people back, will pro'bly pay this undertaker back before this day is done. Joy's fell off to sleep again. Automatic as the arm on a jukebox, I lay my hand on her chest to see if she's still breathing, while watching one of the undertaker's helpers turn a crank at the head of the casket and Mama's head raising up on her pillow of white satin.

Aunt Annie Bell and Aunt Rosanne, at the same time, say, "What the . . . !" Aunt Annie Bell goes to moaning. Aunt Inez, behind her, rubs her shoulders. The rest of us just sets there, dumbstruck.

"What do they think this is?" Aunt Annie Bell whispers. "A colored funeral?"

Mama looks like she's being offered up to glory, and again I've got to say my aunts is got every right to be riled. (This "showing off the corpse" trick, to put it blunt, is what the coloreds around here do at funerals.) I wonder if the undertaker has used this trick casket out of spite, or if Earl has ordered it special out of love for a big to-do.

Aunt Annie Bell gets up and clip-clops in her black patent high heels to the casket, trembling with her white handkerchief over her mouth. Fur stole dragging on the cement floor behind her, like a tail. Black silk dress rustling against her corset, and stockings rasping together with enough friction to set her whole body afire. Everybody standing in the aisle figgers she's leading the line to the casket, and start trailing in behind her. She whirls around, slings her fur stole over one shoulder, and makes a beeline for the pallbearers' pew—one ringed, red-nailed hand held out behind her to halt the feller cranking the head of the casket. "To whom should I express my gratitude?" she says, stopping before the pallbearers with her ice eyes melting.

Buster sets up on the edge of the pew and grabs her other hand, rubbing it. Then, with all the humbleness he can muster, says, "Me, Annie Bell. You didn't think I'd set back and let your sweet sister not be put away proper."

Aunt Annie Bell's hand, held out behind, swings round like a hatchet and chops him across the neck. He lays over on Earl and crooks both arms over his head. Earl just sets there, stiff and red-faced, shoring up Buster.

Ain't a soul in the church house making a peep, and up till now they been study mumbling and shuffling. The line going by the casket stops, all eyes on the fight.

Aunt Rosanne, on her feet now, prances over and steps between Aunt Annie Bell and Buster. "We don't have to resort to violence, sister," she says. "We'll take legal action; we'll sue this . . . this bastard for defamation of character." Looks like she's talking to Buster, who don't never look out from behind his arms.

I hear somebody behind me sniggering, look around and see Aunt Ida Mae, setting scrub-faced and satisfied with her arms crossed.

The undertaker goes over and takes Aunt Rosanne by the arm. She shakes him off like a snake. "All rise," he says and raises his arms again. We all stand up—Pee Wee and Buck blocks my view—and I hear shoes scraping on cement and Aunt Annie Bell quarreling and finally Buster blurting something about the county. He always takes credit for the good and gives the county credit for the bad: say, a dirt ramp holds up, he done it; but if it caves in under a school-bus load of younguns, the county done it.

To get the line going again, Miss Lizabeth steps to the front and starts singing "Precious Memories," and everybody files from back to front, past the casket and out the side door on the right into the streaming gray rain. One out of ten don't even look at Mama; they look at the wrastling match that must be going on between my aunts and Buster, from the sound of scuffling and hissing, even cussing.

Joy comes alive and starts squalling. I stand there, rocking her, watching Mama pumped up on her white satin pillow. "Precious Memories" don't make me cry, like I'd thought. I stand mulling it all over: what-all and who-all brung us to this minute, from the time of Great-Uncle John to the time of Joy.

I see Pee Wee's hand go up to his eyes. Buck starts sniveling. The old man is cackling and jangling cocoaler caps in his pockets.

Jesus wept and I don't blame him.

Alamand

It's raining regular now, pecking sweet on the tin roof and kissing the dirt outside the window. Rain shadows on the windowpanes streak down the walls, my hands. If I was to look now, with the light watery like this, I could make out every pencil marking. But I'm scared to.

The courthouse and the post office, both flat-topped and new, don't call for much redoing. I feel like I oughta do something to the jalousie windows to make them look more real—a crack or something, maybe some boy outside on the grass chunking a rock. But new brick buildings don't call for no such. If I was doing the old biscuit-white, two-story courthouse, I could get away with it. The new one is what it is and don't call for no action. On the other courthouse, the old one, I could put all the old men on the long wood bench of the porch.

That reminds me to go back to the storefront across 129 and put the bench there—that's where they moved it to when they tore the old courthouse down—with three men setting on it. I like drawing them three old characters so much that when I get to the next corner of the room, and my picture of the Methodist Church, I'm hot. The church ain't lacking the way I thought it might be. The Methodists keep it up real good anyhow, but I take down the old steeple and put up a new one with a oversized bell tipped to one side to show it's ringing. So real you can almost hear it. My pencil point is holding up fine. I'm shading in . . . God, it's good!

The bell rings.

I'm really good! I don't care who sees this picture now; I want them to see it. I want to see it myself. I don't look. I'm gone wait till I'm done, and I know it's getting close time for the funeral. I won't quit. Mama would understand. They all would. This is important, important for all of them, me getting the whole town down on these walls.

I feel weak with the weight of the lie.

Just like I thought, the houses both sides of the highway, from the Methodist Church and the courthouse up to the schoolhouse, looks like storybook pictures. I'm fixing them right, real. No more phony crap! Taking my time. It's got to be after three and no need trying to make it to the funeral now. I'll punish myself for missing it by making myself fill in every detail: pumphouses, missing shingles, dangling boards on the sides of houses. I take time to sharpen both pencils, watching the shavings drift to the papers under my feet to keep from looking around at the walls. The rats see the whole picture now. Almost whole, that is.

Earl

— — — — — — — — — — —All I can think is, if I
had me a Kodak I'd get somebody to take a picture of me
and Buster setting here together, shoulder to shoulder, and
that great big old gussied-up woman bowing up at us, fixing to beat the fire out of me or Buster one. When I see it's
him, I don't feel no relief. Except that maybe, just maybe,
Loujean'll give him the credit and the blame.

I'd like a picture of me in this yellow shirt I bought to
court Loujean in, and me selling my Old Timer to Roman
Candle and me feeding everlast dime into that hungry
telephone. I'd like a picture of me bailing off the bridge
into Little River, and me bedding land on top of the
Alapaha River to get out of going to school. And me
sleeping cold in my rat nest all these past many nights last
winter.

I'd like a picture of this whole mess and how it come
to be, and a picture of all these pretty flowers, and one of
love and what it means. Puppy love. I'd like a picture of
the puppy.

Old Man

Undertaker's sweating by the time he runs everybody past Louella's casket and gets her loaded up to haul to the graveyard. Annie Bell and Rosanne both's still raring at Buster till they get in their car and shet the doors. Talk about two sassy old biddies!

What with everybody gaping at them and Buster, while doing their dead-level best to keep their minds on mourning, nobody don't see me slip out of the crowd and squat down behind the cedars on the south side of the church. I watch them all, like turkeys in the rain, running to their automobiles. Watch the undertaker and that piss-poor sheriff trying to get them all going in the right direction. Watch Buster, frazzled, crank up his truck and list right, then left, for a couple of yards with his tire rubber flopping. He stops, face like hit belongs on a fifty-cent piece, and sets waiting for the cars and trucks behind to go on around him and up the muddy road. Guess he don't want to get out and try to flag nobody down and him looking like a hog's been dog-caught.

Through the slow-driving rain, I see him brace his arms on the steering wheel and watch the last car go on around his old blue camper truck and fade out in the rain up ahead. He gets out—his wet-blond hair's sticking up, the knot of his necktie looks like a goiter on the back of his neck—and walks around the front of his truck to the right side. Looks at one tire, then the other, goes to the back, and sights along the low side like he plum expected hit.

"Shit!" he says and hooks his thumbs in his coat pockets.

I come on out then, creeping toward him. He's turned the other way, scratching his head. He checks his watch, maybe figgering if he can make hit to the graveyard in time for the burial.

I step up beside him. "You got a flat, hain't you, Buster?"

He jerks around. "You sonofabitch!" he says and squats down, looking up under the truck.

"You got ery spare?" I say, squatting with him.

Face to face, he stares at me. He's scratched up worser than I thought. One of his gourd eyes is blood-red where a fingernail must've gouged hit.

"Well, I tell you," I say, standing up and leaning on the tailgate. "I got all the feelings in the world for you."

"You sonofabitch!" He stands up.

"I do!" I straighten his necktie.

He yanks away.

"One thing you don't want to mess up and do is get that Annie Bell with something against you."

He walks off to the other side of the truck. "How come?" he says.

"Well, I tell you how come," I say, follering. "For one thing, she's mean."

He rubs his neck where hit looks like a wildcat got holt of him. "That Rosanne's the bitch!"

I laugh. "She's a tiger," I say. "But Annie Bell's the one with the pull."

"The pull?"

"GBI," I say.

"GBI?"

"GBI."

"What about the GBI?" he says.

"You hain't heared?"

"No."

"I thought everybody knowed Annie Bell's with the GBI."

"How's that?"

"She's a bona fide GBI agent."

He leans on the open door a minute, then gets in and cranks the truck. "I hear you!" he says.

"Yep," I say, "she's been regular calling back and to, to Etlanna, checking in and reporting ever since she got here." I poke my head through the window and smell his worryation like something wild.

He shuts off the truck, sets looking out the windshield. "Calling from the phone booth?"

"Regular."

"I think I seen her last night while I was waiting on somebody out there."

"Yeah," I say. "Seems like she got wind of something about the Ku Klux Klan."

He locks eyes with me. "Lord no!" I say, holding up

both hands. "Not me, not that—I didn't say nothing."

He laughs. "I didn't think so. Not and you the one stuck the match to the crib."

"You the one poured the kerosene."

"You helped hold him down."

"I weren't even in there!" I feel like I've let up somewhere and he's fixing to get a holt.

"You ain't got no way a-proving that," he says. His close-set Scurvy eyes look like they get closer.

"Blood's thicker than water," I say, hoping hit'll hold.

Rain is drizzling down the windshield he's looking through. I go on: "I hain't got nothing to lose by painting a picture of you with a hammer in your hand, nails between your teeth, that poor old black c-sucker setting there with his nutsack flopped on the floor."

"I hear you." He's sweating now around drops of rain on his scraped face.

I can't give him no slack. I reach in and twist his BUSTER FOR COMMISSION button straight. He looks at hit, at me. His chin kind of rolls in with his neck.

"You blackmailing sonofabitch!" he says. "I ain't for shore and certain Annie Bell's no GBI agent."

"You hain't for shore and certain she hain't neither," I say. "Now are you?" He just sets there, and I know I gotta do some fast guessing and hope I'm right. "She got real innerstid in that bunch of boys piling in back of this truck last night while she was in the phone booth calling Etlanna."

He don't say nothing.

I'm close. "She's took a real shine to old Earl—you know how he is."

"If he told her I made him do it, he's a lie." He hits the steering wheel with his stubby hands.

"This morning, he just come in dragging, him and Pee Wee and Buck and Alamand. She shore made over them. Set them down and had a heart-to-heart talk with them. Put what they said down on paper."

"Promise them anything?" he asked.

"Something," I say. "I was out and in, tore up over the old lady but . . ."

Buster cackles. "I hear you, Lay Scurvy, you lying sonofabitch!"

I go to itching, feel like I've just about used up what sense I got and my Injun blood's all is left. "Money," I say, looking over the top of the cab where my knuckles is knocking. "You know how people is—money talks."

"Them boys knows better," he says.

"They hain't got nothing to lose."

He raises his pulled-together blond eyebrows at me. "She pays for information?"

"Yeah, all kinds," I say. "Undertaking fraud, county-commissioning fraud, moonshining fraud—you know, like lead poisoning in the quarters and cheating Uncle Sam out of his cut. Ku Klux Klanning, youngun-ruining . . . what you call hit?"

"Contributing to the delinquency of a minor."

"Yeah," I say.

"Buck and Pee Wee ain't . . ."

"You know how people get when they leave home and get city idears," I say, keeping the line tight. "They come back and start trying to fix stuff to suit them. Alamand's Annie Bell's own nephew," I add.

"You shitting me, Lay Scurvy." He grins at me.

"I hain't shitting you," I say. "You denying being in cahoots with the undertaker on Becky's special-built casket?"

"I might of made a little off that trade"——he holds up a stubby pointer finger——"but . . ."

"What about nailing that nigger's nutsack to the crib floor?"

"Me and you both was in on that." He pets my hand on the door.

"I stuck the match to that crib cause me and you both knows back then I had to do what you said or get out. . . ."

"Get out and get a job!" He blows in my face.

"Running shine for you the rest of my natural born days!" I holler.

A drove of little nigger younguns wander past the truck, gazing back with black-grape eyes.

"Git out from here!" Buster slaps the truck door, and they scatter, kicking up mud in the puddles.

I'm too mad and too hot to make sense; I just try to make sentences. "If you don't let Earl and them boys off, I'm telling what-all I know. You can count on hit."

"Who's gone believe you over me?"

"Annie Bell," I say, hoping lies don't show in your eyes like my old man used to say. "She's a outsider looking in."

"Earl owes the county," Buster says, "not me."

"You see if you can't pay the county back then, out of your own pocket," I say. "And call hit fair and square, you hear?"

"I hear you! I hear you!"

"Now git out," I say.

He opens up the door and stomps through the mud to

the back of the truck, pokes his head under the camper top and pulls out a jack. I snatch him around, facing me, and knee him in the nuts. He drops the jack and doubles over, kneeling in the mud.

"I thought you was fixing to help me change my tires," he squalls.

"You got one more flat." I bend down and jerk off his lectioneering button and chunk hit over the wire fence at my back. "You done with county commissioning," I say. "Scurvys hain't gone be hoodooed out of what's coming to them no more?"

He lifts his face and muddy slobber's running down his chin. "Louella's still a pauper," he says, still on his knees, still holding his nuts. "The last pauper in Swanoochee County."

I go to sock him, he dodges. I walk off up the road in the rain. "If the county takes over Louella's funeral bill, she really is the last pauper," he hollers like hits his'try now.

"I hear you," I say, walking, proud to give up my pride for his'try.

Alamand

——————————————— I go on drawing: rotten boards, warped eaves, scaling paint. I go on, standing on my stool now, and open up the road to Buster's house and the shortcut where the school buses run, and do the houses along that stretch—my arm's aching bad—and the hotel.

It's big, spreading out and moving close to the courthouse, not too close though, with a road elbowing from 129 to 94. Every window of the old hotel knocked out by rocks; people all inside, you can't see; but their clothes are hung out over the banisters on the dipping top gallery. A youngun's tricycle on the bottom gallery, so many doors. Half open. Tufts of grass in the sandy yard. Buster's chinaberry tree giving shade to two backyards, across from the schoolhouse. Sunspots in the shade of oaks. So many people have lived in the old hotel, but nobody lives here now. Doesn't matter. They used to. Should it still be the same season as now if the picture is of people who used to live here . . . there? I'll leave it, because it is good. God says, It *was* good.

Satisfied anyhow, I go on up the road, working 94 and

the shortcut at the same time, wearing down my pencil lead on sidewalks and blacktop, up to the schoolhouse. Lord, I want to look now! I know this is the best picture I ever done, the most real. I want Earl to see it. That's real good, he'd say, but he wouldn't really understand it. Wouldn't really see what it is, all the old and new, the real and unreal. . . .

I open up 94 east to Tarver and let all that old/new, real/unreal crap go. I shouldn't try to make it click. If it's good, it just is, and I know it's good. If I look, I might not know it anymore. And I need to know something more than just the fact that I've messed around and missed my own mama's funeral.

My mama is dead and I won't never see her no more.

The schoolhouse keeps me busy. The angles of the old building, all the add-ons. New classrooms, flat-top brick, along 94, just like the courthouse. I go on and do them just like they are, new and perfect, just like I'd eat to keep going even when I ain't hungry.

I can already see younguns' footprints in the sandy school yard, so I lead off with them to the old part of the schoolhouse and fix it right: windows big as doors, the old breezeway hooking old to new buildings, the old auditorium with its scrolled-arch doorway. I put cigarette butts all up under the smoking tree and a bunch of tough-looking boys standing in the circle shade—nobody I know good, just boys I know of around Cornerville.

On the playground, between the old and new wings of the school, I draw the whirl-a-way spinning two little boys with their hands gripping the bars. One big boy, like Buck, is grinning mean and running around in the kicked-out dirt trench, pushing the whirl-a-way fast. Again, I use double lines to show the action. Looks like it'll spin up to the sun, which I draw just over the oak with the teachers' bench built around it. I put a teacher on the bench with her head bowed and a open book on her lap—and a apple, which has been drawed about a million times before, but I like it so I keep it. The sun is too ragged from me trying to show it shining by making marks around it. I might have to erase it and let the oak shadows do the trick.

Buster'll pro'bly tear Aunt Becky's house down anyhow.

I reach high and draw the baseball diamond on the south end of the playground, where the road from the quarters hooks all the way round. I give the trees some roots and moss and dead limbs. That's good. The roots look a little too much like snakes though.

I have a time on the colored people's shanties, since they do look alike, all built in the same shotgun style. But what I put around them, junk and all, makes up for it. I do have to make up stuff though. Except at old Lucious's house; I do it real. A little more square-built, bigger, than the others. His old well, out back, the lopsided outhouse, the trash pile. I know it's the wrong season, winter, but I put a cluster of prince's-feathers in the gully where the water from his watershelf cuts across the left side of the packed-sand yard.

And then it comes to me: old Lucious could be a African prince. So for the heck of it, I make him one. Who cares? I make his rocker into a throne and him setting watch over the road where a bunch of younguns is playing on a old inner tube (not just like the flower picture

I did before). I make Lucious a crown, fancy with tiny perfect jewels in it, a circle of prongs on top. Make his hair bushed out around his strong face. Big gold teeth showing. (One time in Tarver he toted a fifty-pound sack of hog feed between his teeth clean across the commissary.) I make him a bright robe—wine as the prince's-feathers in my head—with lines on each side to show it shining. Bare feet flat on the wide-board floor. Hands folded in his lap. I make his shoulders fatter, rounder, higher, his head too, and I know he don't look real, but I don't care. I can't think about what everybody will think when they see him like this. They're pro'bly thinking pretty bad of me right now anyway for not showing up at my own mama's funeral.

I'm at the church now.

Loujean

——————————————————————**W**inding back through
the quarters to the turnoff at the old school, Aunt Annie
Bell clicks her tongue with the windshield wipers. *Nck nck
nck.* Still all to pieces from her run-in with Buster.

The car rings with Joy's crying, and every so often
Aunt Annie Bell speeds up, then hits the brakes just short
of plowing into the back of the hearse.

I keep my eyes on Mama's casket through the windshield
while I change Joy's dirty diaper and try to stop her suck bottle rolling on the floor with my foot, at the same time covering her wagging head so the cold rain slashing through Aunt
Rosanne's open window don't give her the earache.

"I declare," says Aunt Rosanne, "I don't know if the
odor is worse out there or in here." She cranks up her window quick.

"Raw sewage and wet dogs." Aunt Annie Bell is driving with both shaking hands on the wheel. She gazes back
at me in the rearview mirror with black-rimmed, watery
blue eyes. "That could have waited," she says. "*Nck nck
nck.*" Meaning Joy messing on herself, I guess.

I stomp down on the suck bottle with my left foot, pinning the wiggling baby down on the seat beside me, reach to the floor, and grab the bottle. Aunt Annie Bell hits the brakes and my left shoulder rams the back of her seat. She glares at me in the mirror again. I poke the nipple in Joy's mouth, she gags on it, then goes to sucking.

"Oh Lord!" says Aunt Rosanne through her teeth, then lays her head back on her mangy fur stole hanging over the seat. "I cannot wait to get out of this place."

"I could use a little R & R myself," says Aunt Annie Bell.

"Florida," Aunt Rosanne says.

R & R, Florida—I listen for clues, guessing the R's stand for restaurants.

"Well," says Aunt Annie Bell to Aunt Rosanne, "you may as well brace yourself, because we'll be here for a while." She butts her head of varnished blond curls toward the back seat. "Remember?" she adds.

Aunt Rosanne eyeballs her. "What about it?"

"We've got to make a decision, one way or the other."

They're talking about the baby, maybe even about me. My God, I'm just sixteen, what if they make me go home with them?

"I thought I'd made myself clear about that," Aunt Rosanne says and sets high.

"Well, what do you suggest then?" Aunt Annie Bell stares at her—car on automatic along the wet stretch of gravel to the red light.

Aunt Rosanne turns halfway round in the seat and says, "Loujean, honey . . ."

"You know better, Rosanne," says Aunt Annie Bell. "She's only a child. *Nck nck nck!*"

"You mean whoever takes the baby should take her?"

To take care of the baby, I think.

"Of course," says Aunt Annie Bell. Her melty eyes pop up in the rearview mirror again. "Loujean?"

"I'm fixing to get married," I blurt out and my brain goes hot with shock.

"Married!" yells Aunt Rosanne. "Why, I never heard of such! Married to who?"

"Earl," I say, biting my top lip. Joy's finished her bottle, so I put her on my shoulder to burp, hoping to head off the colic. I watch the red light, coming up quick, watch Aunt Annie Bell with her eyes on Aunt Rosanne. "Look out!" I holler.

She brakes—"Who's Earl?"—easing off the bumper of the hearse and driving on through the red light, where Deputy Saul stands in his drenched blue uniform with his hat over his heart.

Who is Earl? How can I tell them who he is? He seems so strong and clear to me, but to them he'd be a fuzzy nobody, one of them boys won't never make nothing out of hisself. Who is Earl? Just a good-hearted old boy. Not somebody you'd pick out in a crowd, not somebody a girl would dream about marrying.

"You don't know him," I say.

"You people!" Aunt Annie clicks her tongue. "Marrying the first person comes along, and at your age!" She gives Aunt Rosanne one of them satisfied looks that says, Aren't you glad we got out of Swanoochee County?

They won't take Joy without me to take care of her. Already they're talking about the sunset from some restaurant window in Key West, while Aunt Rosanne scrubs the matted spot on her fur stole like she's washing it. I bet they'll go to fighting before they get to the Florida line. Aunt Rosanne might even try to steal Aunt Annie Bell's stole again.

"Stealing stoles," I say out loud and laugh, glad I am who I am, and they don't even hear me.

It's slacked off raining. I hug the baby to me and she nods off to sleep as we come in view of the cement river bridge where a girl, looks like Sonia Lee, is standing on the other side—one knee cocked in dungarecs, a blue canvas pack on her back, thumb stuck out like she's hitchhiking west. We turn right, this side of the bridge, onto the dirt ramp leading to the cemetery: white tombstones gleaming in the rainy light and a clump of green cedars poking from the middle of the packed wet sand. Frogs croak from the riverbanks behind the cemetery, where tupelos, gums, and pines reach to the bluing sky.

I always wanted to go to Florida, but not in my aunts' back seat. I bet if I was to tell Earl I wanted to go, he'd take me, one way or the other. I bet if I was to tell Earl I said I was fixing to marry him, he'd marry me. I won't. My aunts don't really care, even though as I crawl out of the back seat at Mama's open grave, Aunt Annie Bell holds her big black umbrella over me and Joy. I can see relief on her tired painted face, and figger my aunts will leave for Florida right after the graveside preaching.

"Thank you," I say.

Alamand

It's raining at the church—
I have to show that. Streaks slanting across the front, across
the cedars along the sides, the shanties all around. There's a
empty steeple on top of the church. I don't give it a bell. It's
a dull day anyhow; a bell won't help. Even if I'd heard a
bell ring, I wouldn't of gone. I don't think they ring bells for
funerals.

It could be over by now.

I go on and put lots of cars at the church, the hearse
too (I'm there now). The front door's open, and I draw
heads and fading shoulders of all the people and just a
glimpse of the casket and flowers through the door. Looks
so real I can hear them singing inside.

I draw Buck's truck, parked out front, one post stan-
dard bent on the back. I'm crying, not because I know I'm
not able and fit to face her funeral like Earl and them, but
because what I'm doing is so important and pro'bly won't
never mean nothing.

I don't even want to look at the picture now.

My eyes is raining tears on the floor like the clouds is

raining water on the ground, and it's all because I'm getting so close to where I really am. I'm at the church house in my picture, and just around the next curve I'm fixing to be where I am. Me and me—I was born with a double veil, they say—coming together at last. On my birthday, on my deathday.

Loujean

_ _ _ _ _ _ _ _ _ _ _ **W**hile the preacher's preaching, at Mama's graveside, I spot Earl on the other side of the fake-grass mat and tip through the crowd to stand next to him. Joy's crying with the colic. Aunt Annie Bell looks across the rainbow bank of flowers at me, and I nod toward Earl. She stares at him, swaying with his hands latched behind. She stares a long time, then shakes her head. I thread my hand through his right elbow, and he places his palm on the stomach of his yellow shirt, like he's escorting me to a prom.

Touching his warm, dry skin, I feel a shock run through me. I don't look at him. I want to think of him like he is, my hero, not cloudy-eyed Earl, always saying the wrong thing. I might marry him someday. The good in him weighs a lot more than the bad. Even that tacky business of pumping up Mama's body at the funeral was done from the heart.

The preacher wraps up with a prayer, and everybody starts milling about and saying stuff they don't mean. I slip off to the stand of cedars, where rain leaks from the needles to the packed sand. Letting Joy exercise her lungs, as Miss Amaretta says. My aunts is hugging everybody and making connections, happy as if they're fixing to eat.

I look for Earl and the boys and can't locate them in the crowd, then hear the post truck crank up. Looks like Earl doing the driving—inching forward and backward, to keep from bumping Aunt Annie Bell's car ahead or Cousin Winston's truck behind, then straightening up and heading along the cemetery road to the highway.

On the run again, I guess.

In a minute, the old man comes switching past the cedar thicket, on his way to the graveside, grinning with his hands in his pockets, and mingles in with the crowd. I got a good notion why he's late, since Buster ain't showed yet. I wonder if he got the best of Buster, if Earl and the boys can come on back to the house. Back to the house where I'll pick up where Mama left off: doing the best I can till I can do better.

Before long, I see the old man kind of hanging back from the crowd, then slipping off around the hearse with his back to the cedar thicket. He stands there, not ten feet from me, watching the crowd over the top of the wet black hearse, then squats down fiddling with the valve stem on the left front tire. I watch the left front dip, then watch him duck-walking toward the back, stop and poke what looks like a match in the valve stem of the left rear tire. While watching the left back tire sink to the packed sand, I lose sight of him, but figger he's on the other side when I see the right rear and then the right front of the hearse settle low and the puddle of light on the roof level out.

I wait for him to show again around the back of the

hearse, maybe let the air out of Aunt Annie Bell's tires. When he don't, I know why. He ain't about to hold my aunts up from leaving now the funeral's done. I smile, pressing my hand on the baby's blanket-tented head, and start walking toward the highway, then home.

Old Man's not the kind to let the air out of just one tire and make it easy on people. He's got to let the air out of all four tires, and until people start carrying around more then one spare, they can't outdo him.

Earl

One time I went with Alamand to the Alapaha bridge to float a old cane-syrup bottle with a message in it downriver. I didn't never ask him what he wrote on that rolled-up tablet paper with blue lines in that scoured bottle with a cork in the neck, and he didn't never tell me. But about a month later, he showed me a letter come in the mail from some man in Tampa, Florida. The letter read: "I found your bottle with the message in it at the mouth of the Suwannee, Gulf of Mexico. And my answer to your question is, I don't know and I don't know anybody else who knows. Maybe you should float the same question in another bottle down another river."

I want to say to Loujean, I don't even know the question, so how can I know the answer?

That autumn morning on the riverbank, south side of the bridge, me and Alamand squatted barefoot on the damp sand and watched the tea-colored water flow from the scalloped shallows, where mussels burrowed with day-moon eyes, to the black eddies and whorls that veed out in a pewter gash between banks of green felt. The sky was Sunday-school-book blue.

We didn't say a word, just watched and listened to the river rushing and the wind risping in the willows and the springs trickling from the steep, rooty banks, upriver and downriver and across the creek-width stream. We listened to the martins wheeping in the bridge girders, and now and then a car passing from seam to seam of the bridge with a measured *woom-shish, woom-shish* sound. We read the painted names of lovers on the cement pylons, and watched a hawk swoop low over the river, crying, and land in a cypress old as God. Oval berries, red as the lovers' names, dropped from the bow-bellied tupelos to the breeze-wrinkled water and drifted down to where Alamand's bottle would go if he was lucky. If it didn't lodge in a flotsam of twigs and driftwood, or snag on a tussock or a moccasin-braided cypress knee. It could end up as just another old bottle on a sandbar between here and there.

Alamand held on to that bottle with both hands for what seemed like forever, then at last he stood and waded out, solemn as a preacher at a baptizing, in his white shirt and blue jeans. Neck-deep, in the middle of the river, with just his white face bobbing like a plastic jug on the black water, he dunked the bottle, testing to see if it would float, if it would leak, if it would go. Eyes on the gash of pewter downriver where it veed out to nothingness, like he wondered if the river really went anywhere.

Maybe that was Alamand's question, or maybe the question in the bottle asked if anybody had seen God, or something as down-to-earth as whether the water or the willows is responsible for the river air's tart smell. Could've been he was just sending out a call for paint.

I was watching his rapt face and missed the high point when he let the bottle go, but I seen it spinning downriver like a trick fish and shrink to about the size of an eye, then vanish into that valley of things lost until found.

Alamand

— — — — — — — — — — **A**ll the time I'm touching up the quarter shanties, coming this away, I'm hurrying, then holding back to keep from getting to the clearing of Aunt Becky's place. I feel me coming like I feel the eyes of the rats.

I'm a lizard on the wall with that white sand drawing me like a warm round sun. I'm soaking it up; it's soaking me up. My pencil makes *pck pck* sounds like the rain on the tin.

I'm crying and the pencil marks look blurry, but I've got to go on. I can't stop now. Sand's drawing me. I get up to the wallowed-down fence of the yard and want to stop, but I don't. I can't. I move on in.

I move on in and work on the outside of the house a little bit, knowing it don't need it, is real enough. I work on the flowers in the circle of dome-glass insulators, making them dead-looking—withered leaves and thistles. To keep away from the well, on the east side of the yard, I work on the treeline behind the well, making the cypress head-up above the pines.

I'm crying hard, a chugging cry, like a car trying to start, the way people crying sound to break your heart.

I go on to the well, work on the crumbling mortar of the outside wall, and think about Earl and how this time he won't be here to help. He's out doing what he has to do, needs to do, living in the real world where I can't, where I've opened up the roads to nowhere for me. It's okay. I don't have to go. Earl will go.

I move on up the well and open up the rim by drawing a half-moon. On the rim, I draw Aunt Becky's squat midget body perched with wings raised instead of arms. Just the toe of her shoes showing from under her long skirts, her frock and pinafore apron. Every freckle on her face I dot; hair sketched back in a bun on her regular-sized head, her eyes spooked wide. That mum mouth.

Now me. Now I draw me. Me at the bottom of the well, where the water is clear and cold and ringing like locusts, a sweet ringing of oblivion punctured by my bellering. I splash, bob, suck water like air, rise up sputtering and grab holt of a jutting brick, hook one set of fingers, one set of toes, crossing over on the bricks going up, slip on the mossy mold along the sides and drop like a rock to the bottom of the well. I start over and over, water dripping off me and warbling like wrens to the pool below, a reminder to hang fast, all ten fingers, all ten toes, numb-cold. I cry, I don't quit—I'm on my own now, how everybody ends up—hollow sounds and green smells like ferns in the wet woods.

When I get close to the top, fixing to latch on to Aunt Becky's skirt and winch myself up to the rim, she flutters her wings and shudders crown to toe and lifts straight up into the circle of blue heavens, wings arched and gliding like a tilly hawk's. Hugging the rough cement rim, I belly up and straddle it and quit crying.

A truck pulls up out front and sets idling; a door opens and snaps to. I hope it's Earl, even if I don't need him now. I hop down off the well and don't try to cover nothing up.

He eases open the front door and steps inside the room. Spies me at the well on the east wall. "Hey, Buddy," he says, stepping around the open door. "We was wondering what went with you." He stops, gazing down at the papers on the floor, then from end to beginning of the picture on the walls. "They're waiting on us in the truck," he adds, tipping over the rug of papers to the well, reaching out, touching it, traveling his hand along the town on the walls.

"Sonofagun!" he says and whistles when he gets to old Lucious, now a African prince, and stands back and laughs.

I laugh with him, scratching my head. "Don't look real, does it?"

"Nope," he says, stepping up like he's checking a statue for cracks.

"I messed up." I kneel in the disturbed nest of papers, and for something to do, shake out and stack them one at a time.

"I like it," he says low, walking on around the room in a daze. Mouth open and hand passing over the schoolhouse, the hotel, the Methodist Church—stopping to look close—then the courthouse.

I feel hot and faint. I start evening the edges of the papers. "I didn't make it, Earl."

"You sure-dog did!" he says. "Look at me! Look at me by the phone booth! Hot-amighty!"

"I meant to the funeral," I say, watching him blow up like a toad frog with pride.

"I ain't never had no picture of myself before," he says.

"Buster'll probably tear this place down," I say.

Earl acts like he don't hear me at first, stands looking at his picture like he's looking in a mirror. "I want to keep it; could be he'll turn it into a packhouse."

I know he don't get the whole picture. He's like most people, wanting a rose to look like a rose, not some image they gotta think about. "All of it ain't real-looking," I say.

"Don't need to be, Bub." He sounds like he's way off, talking to hisself. "If it was we couldn't take it."

"Honest to God?" I say.

"Honest to God." He turns around. His face looks blanched in the gray light, more sober than I ever seen it. He walks over and squats down before me. At first, I figger he's sorry for me, then see in his eyes he's not, he's surprised at me. I feel new.

"I should of gone to the funeral," I say.

He shrugs. "If you needed to."

We both look at the picture of the church house in the quarters. He knows I've had her funeral right here. What he doesn't know is I've had mine too.

The next paper I pick up happens to be the sunflower picture I drawed away back of the colored younguns on the inner tube. I press it smooth with my hands and pass it to him.

"Keep it for a souvenir," I say and keep on shuffling papers like I don't care where he do or don't.

He holds it up to the light of the window. His forehead wrinkles up. He studies it from all sides, and ends up holding it like he's reading a letter. "I knowed you was a good hand to draw," he says, "but . . ." His earnest blue eyes linger along the walls, from beginning to end of the picture, like there's always more to read into it.

"I might get me some paint and paint over it," I say, gazing with him at the whole thing. I wouldn't paint over it for nothing.

"No," he says. "Leave it like it is. Leave it for us to remember by."